KAMYONISTAN REVEALED

KAMYONISTAN REVEALED

ROBERT HACKFORD

ATHENA PRESS
LONDON

KAMYONISTAN REVEALED
Copyright © Robert Hackford 2008

All Rights Reserved

No part of this book may be reproduced in any form
by photocopying or by any electronic or mechanical means,
including information storage or retrieval systems,
without permission in writing from both the copyright
owner and the publisher of this book.

ISBN: 978 1 84748 442 0

First published 2008 by
ATHENA PRESS
Queen's House, 2 Holly Road
Twickenham TW1 4EG
United Kingdom

Printed for Athena Press

Also by Robert Hackford:

Kamyonistan

Kamyonistan Revisited

Kamyonistan Long-Haul Services

Kamyonistan Long-Haul Services was a well-established Middle-East freight forwarder. It operated from an office in the freight agency building adjoining Kamyonistan's impressive truck stop, which had been constructed in the style of a medieval caravanserai, complete with stone walls and minarets. The company had its own special set of rules. It ran no vehicles of its own, but organised the movement of freight to and from the Middle East from all over Europe, North Africa and Central Asia. It offered continuous work at very attractive rates to owner-drivers and operators of small fleets. However, all vehicles had to run in KLHS livery. This consisted of plain white for the cabs of tractor units; and yellow canopies with violet side boards for tilt trailers. Refrigerated trailers were painted yellow. All trailers had KAMYONISTAN LONG-HAUL SERVICES stencilled in black capital letters to both sides. In the relaxed culture of Middle-East transport, this was highly unusual, but livery costs were defrayed by the company and this in turn proved to be a highly successful publicity device. Also unusual, for the Middle East, was the extensive use of tilts. KLHS specified tilts in ninety per cent of its work. This was partly because some of any given cargo's journey was spent crossing Europe. The remaining ten per cent of its work was divided between temperature-controlled freight and container transport.

Surprisingly, for a company that made such precise demands concerning trailer type and livery, KLHS did not specify the make, age or condition of the tractor units to be used. Consequently, the work was performed by units representing just about every manufacturer to have created lorries since the sixties. It was the same with trailers. Just as Volvo F88s ran alongside Volvo FH16s, so pitch-roofed 12 metre tilts ran alongside 13.6 metre tilts with sliding canopies. Poor drivers were able to work with wealthy ones throughout the region, but only those with modern vehicles were permitted into Europe. Drivers from all over the Middle East, from the Gulf to Turkey, operated in the distinctive livery. Some of them ran desert spec 6 x 6 Titan units with high ground-clearance trailers. The franchise system had recently begun to prove very popular with foreign owner-drivers from Europe; especially those who had previously enjoyed the Middle-East run, but who had been disappointed when the work dried up because of low haulage rates.

In consequence of the recent rocket attack upon Kamyonistan by jittery Israeli forces, the Syrian transport zone had suffered a crisis of confidence. Some companies, like the clothing factory that sent consignments of workwear to Britain, and the Paradise Restaurant situated in the truck stop, maintained a sturdy optimism for the future of the zone. Others, however, had lost their nerve and had put their premises up for sale at the earliest opportunity. One of these had been a small haulage firm called Kamyonistan-TIR. This outfit was of little consequence to KLHS because it was not interested in running a fleet of lorries. Their premises, however, attracted KLHS's attention the moment it appeared on the market because it included a modest container terminal. It had suffered minor damage during the rocket attack but was otherwise ready for work. Its proprietor sold the whole outfit for 'a song', and its new owners moved in immediately.

This small and perfectly formed container terminal was a Middle-East transport entrepreneur's dream. For one thing, the yard was self-contained, with workshops, offices and warehouses. For another, it had a huge parking area with fuel facilities. It also had its own forklift trucks and a top-loader capable of carrying laden shipping containers. There was space to stack containers, served by two gantry cranes for transferring containers from one line to another. A motley collection of trailers comprised a mixture of purpose-built skeletal container carriers, platform trailers fitted with twist-locks and cut-down desert trailers. It was hoped that the newly acquired terminal at Kamyonistan would handle KLHS's own growing stock of liveried shipping containers. In addition, it would serve as an excellent operating base for many of their subcontractors, offering transhipping facilities and warehousing.

The reappearance of Ro and Nuri in Kamyonistan had surprised nobody. Ro, an English youth and Nuri, an Egyptian one, had become a vital part of the community's history in recent years. Temporary accommodation was arranged for them at the little-patronised motel in the truck stop. Indeed, the personnel manager at Kamyonistan Long-Haul Services had been quick to recruit Ro and Nuri, now aged seventeen, as 'runners' for their old office in the freight agency building next door. Because of the rocket attack, the transport zone had been failing to attract workers from nearby Damascus, so the same serendipity that had radically altered the fortunes of Kamyonistan Long-Haul Services also handed the kind of security and employment to Ro and Nuri that would not normally have been available. They were both very familiar and comfortable with Kamyonistan, and between them they spoke English, Arabic and a smattering of Turkish. As they were young, bright, potentially excellent employees, the personnel manager had pulled enough strings and paid sufficient baksheesh to obtain work permits and visas for them. This was no mean feat, even in Syria, but the truth was that KLHS was in the process of becoming a very influential company.

A month or so into his new employment at Kamyonistan Long-Haul Services, Nuri extracted a sheaf of papers from the feeder tray of the freight agency photocopier and went to his little desk to put them in order. He had paperwork for a Turkish KLHS driver and a release note for a Syrian driver who had come to collect one of the container trailers. The little office was hot, and he was glad to get out into the fresh breeze that blew off the mountain. Crossing the TIR-parking compound, he squinted against the bright sunlight which illuminated little eddies of dust in his path. He enjoyed his work and the sense of purpose that it provided, not to mention the salary. However, he was missing Ro.

Ro had been despatched with one of the newly defected Iranian drivers to Baku in Azerbaijan. Just before the big takeover, Kamyonistan-TIR had been offered a lucrative little job transporting oilfield equipment to a rig-blast yard near the capital. It had been decided by the office to send it by shipping container. Then they had problems obtaining the correct visa for the Syrian driver, so they chose to send one of the Iranian drivers instead. The driver's mate was also Syrian, and he too could not get a visa. In the end, they elected to send Ro as 'trailer boy' and the appropriate visas were procured. Nuri was a little put out because Ro had been told that if he conducted himself well, he would be sent on further interesting journeys. Nuri, on the other hand, had been informed in no uncertain terms that only having one arm disqualified him from such expeditions. Notwithstanding this setback, the boy who had been struck by lightning remained pretty upbeat in his approach to the daily routine of bearing paperwork from trucks to the office and back.

Meanwhile, among the tangle of giant metal structures that littered the bleak rig-blast yard of a Baku oil terminal, Ro was helping to close the rear doors of the rusty container. Beyond their lorry lay the lurid, turquoise Caspian Sea. Rashid, the driver, had been filling Ro in about the country they were visiting. 'Azerbaijan is an Islamic country,' he said. 'Once it was part of Persia, then it fell to the Russians. It contains much of the Caucasus mountain range that we saw on the way here. This empty container is going to rattle like a drum on these atrocious roads!'

Ro checked the tyres down the nearside while Rashid did the offside, before climbing into the thirty-year-old Mercedes, which was a New Generation 2032 with its distinctive black breather pipe running up the side of the cab. It was stifling inside, and Rashid turned on the roof-mounted air conditioning, but the machine was old and fighting a losing battle. In the end they simply opened the windows again. 'It's a pity the new company saw fit to sell off those Eurotrakkers we brought from Iran,' Rashid grumbled. 'They were far newer than these Mercs!'

'Why did they sell them, then?' Ro asked.

'Kamyonistan Long-Haul Services has a policy of never actually owning a lorry. It keeps the overheads down. These old Mercs will be sold off to subbies to be painted up in KLHS colours,' Rashid explained.

'Will you buy one?'

'No!' Rashid laughed. 'I can't afford to.'

The battered old lorry picked its way among the cranes, winches, tanks and gantries of the vast site. To Ro, it resembled a scrapyard the size of a small town. 'What I like about these places is that you never, ever see tourists in them. Only drivers see this sort of place,' Ro said.

Rashid laughed. 'You're right,' he said. 'One of the things that makes travel by lorry unique is that many parts of the Middle-East TIR trail do not coincide with the package tourist trail, or even with the overlanders' trail. Adventure tourists' overland vehicles can occasionally be found in truck stops and embarkation parks at ports, but the industrial zones and areas of rural commerce are the domains of truckers alone.'

They crashed and ground along rutted roads where water buffalo roamed among the hissing samovars of wayside *chai* sellers. From time to time their progress was impeded by herds of sheep being driven through the jumble of melon stalls that crowded the edges of the road. A curious mixture of Turkish and Russian music wailed from the little markets, which served to remind Ro that Azerbaijan was both Middle Eastern and Central Asian.

As the sun hung above a violet landscape in the early evening, Rashid steered the old Merc into a TIR park situated in an arid bowl set into the hills. Ganja TIR park was one of those epic, walled Turkish-run truck stops. It was nearly empty, so Rashid took the opportunity of filling up with cheap diesel at the filthy pumps, while a hot wind blew dust across the rugged terrain from the south. After cautioning Ro not to swallow any of the shower water, they cleaned themselves up before entering the restaurant. The room was hung with Turkish carpets. *Chai* was a self-service affair that involved attaching a loop of live wire to the kettle while trying to avoid electrocution. Chicken kebabs provided sustenance.

The following day began with the relocation of an air tank that had come adrift on the rough roads. After that, they braved the road to the Georgian border, which they cleared without too much drama because the trailer was empty; but for reasons best known to the local police, they were not permitted to travel until the next day.

Everything in Georgia appeared to be derelict and abandoned. The countryside, however, was a paradise of fronds and fritillaries, and eventually they arrived at the customs post at Kutaisi. Later, the road degenerated further as they dodged cows and pigs that wandered in their path. In the afternoon, they began to descend a winding hill to the coast. Misty crags hung above colonial-style bungalows among dripping palms and lush vegetation.

Arriving in the Black Sea port of Batumi, they were reduced to walking pace by the wrecked road surfaces. Dodging potholes, Rashid pointed at derelict buildings and sagging wires. Livestock wandered in the markets where road signs were written in Roman, Georgian or Cyrillic script or in all three. Overtaking buses that belched black smoke, they left the city. The sky grew dark and violet lightning flickered over the sea. They stopped that night at the Turkish border town of Sarpi.

Turkey seemed like a breath of fresh air next morning. As they bowled along the sun-drenched Black Sea coast road that dipped and dived into the tea-growing region, Rashid sang Iranian songs.

'Do you miss Iran?' Ro asked.

'No. At least, I don't miss the Iran we have today,' Rashid said firmly. 'That's why I defected. Do you miss England?'

'No,' said Ro. 'I miss Nuri. He's my friend; I'll be glad to get back to him.'

'I think we'd better follow the prescribed TIR route,' Rashid said, heading inland to follow the road to Bayburt and Askale. This road took them over some serious mountains, affording relief-map views of eastern Turkey. The going was good and the scenery dramatic. 'Great in fair weather,' Rashid said, 'but this isn't a road to be on with a lorry in winter!'

At midday they lunched in a café at Askale, on kebabs and salad washed down with the yoghurt drink known as *ayran*. Here, they joined the east–west route used by Iranians. Rashid pointed out the Iranian trucks with their outsized tyres, but he was careful not to raise a hand in salutation lest he be recognised. He was, after all, an exile. Ro, who had received a little tuition in his uncle's ERF, asked Rashid about the Mercedes and its controls. 'When we find somewhere quiet, I'll let you discover for yourself,' Rashid said. 'Perhaps when we get back to Damascus.'

At Erzincan TIR post they called it a day, and after having their police paper stamped, they went into a packed restaurant for grilled fish and Turkish beer. Most of the trucks parked there were Turkish though a few were Bulgarian. However, at least four of them were Iranian and Rashid became very agitated. Ro noted the Iranian DAF 3600 and three Scania Streamliners standing in the corner. As soon as his meal was over, Rashid repaired to the cab, leaving Ro to sip *chai* in front of a televised football match.

When the match was over, Ro sauntered back to the wagon. He knew that something was wrong as he approached it. Both cab doors were wide open and clothes and papers from inside were strewn about under the wheels. Clearly, there had been a struggle. By the dim light cast from the cab roof through the open driver's door, Ro saw blood on the asphalt. At that moment, an air horn blasted from the gate. In the glare of their headlamps he witnessed the dusty departure of the four Iranian trucks into the night. Throwing what he could back into the cab, Ro removed the keys, locked the doors and went to find help. He got the distinct impression that he probably would not be seeing Rashid again.

No stranger to living in lorries, Ro settled in for a long wait. The police had spent half the night questioning him, while the cab was subjected to forensic inspection. If the sun had not been so fierce the next morning, Ro might have slept until midday. As it was, he arose mid-morning, swept out the cab and speculated about whether or not the old girl would live long enough to be painted in Long-Haul white. Then he went for Turkish coffee. It was not available. He was informed that Turkish truckers could not afford Turkish coffee, so he settled for *chai*. The previous evening, an officer had put him through to the transport manager, Fahmy, who had told Ro to stay put until a driver could be found to retrieve the lorry. If necessary, he had said, he would come himself. Ro liked Fahmy; he was loud, jolly and had a good sense of humour. He had reminded Ro to run the engine each day to 'keep her interested'. Fahmy's future was uncertain because when the last tractor was sold, he would have no lorries left to manage. Perhaps Fahmy would buy up the battered Merc, Ro thought.

It was while Ro was running the motor that he received a visit from a pair of plain-clothed officers. They asked him about what he knew of Rashid's defection. 'I only know that he defected. I don't know any more than that,' Ro said. 'Will they kill him?'

'They would have smuggled him into Iran if we hadn't caught them,' the officer said.

'You've found him, them?' Ro said, relieved.

'Yes. Thanks to your description of the Iranian *kamyons*, we've taken your friend into safe keeping. The drivers are probably fairly innocent, but their so-called assistants are Intelligence personnel and are really tricky customers. Even now, we may be powerless to prevent them from taking Rashid to Iran. Either way, I doubt if he will be returning to Syria.' The plain-clothed officers, who told Ro that Rashid had asked them to ensure Ro's safety, took him for lunch before leaving him to doze in the afternoon sunshine.

The Turkish driver who turned up to collect the Mercedes had not been told to expect a passenger, and he was none too pleased to find Ro on board. His disposition could only be described as 'sullen'. Ro gave up trying to talk to him after the first few miles. When they arrived at Çilvegozu, the Turkish side of the Syrian border a day and half later, the Turk abandoned the truck and hitched a ride with a Turkish truck going home. Ro telephoned the office. Fahmy reassured him that a relief driver was on his way. The relief driver turned up in a Turkish police car. It was Rashid.

'They've told me not to leave Syria again,' Rashid said as he stuffed the vehicle paperwork against the windscreen and fired up the engine. 'They're right! I was a fool to attempt an international run so soon after defecting. Now of course Intelligence knows that I'm alive and that I wasn't killed in the rocket attack.' He drove along the wild road through the hills of 'no-man's-land' to the Syrian side of the border at Bab al Hawa – the Gate of Winds.

Ro asked, 'Will you be safe now?'

'No! Worse still, now that they know that I'm alive, it won't be rocket science to work out that the others are alive and that they've probably defected as well. The depressing part is that I've endangered my colleagues,' Rashid said, miserably.

'How did they find you out, though?'

'They didn't! One of the agents riding shotgun with the Iranian drivers recognised me. He had been present in Tehran when I was loading those containers for Kamyonistan. They were top priority military loads travelling incognito – or at least, they were supposed to be. Nothing's very private any more, with those satellites floating about in the heavens.'

'You'll have to do local runs, then,' Ro said.

'If KLHS retire this knackered lorry but want it as a yard shunter, I might offer to buy it cheaply and play with container skellies all day,' Rashid mused.

'Inshallah,' Ro put in.

'Inshallah,' Rashid said, with feeling.

'Where are we eating tonight? Homs convoy stop?' Ro asked, relishing the thought of revisiting this fine example of a Middle-East truck stop.

'Yes! And the meal is on me, son. I understand that the detailed descriptions of the Iranian wagons that you gave to the police almost certainly saved my life,' Rashid said. 'Or from a fate worse than death,' he added, darkly.

Kamyonistan Regained

Kamyonistan had a new air about it. A sense of purpose prevailed in the commercial community. Premises that had closed after the rocket attack were opened up to let the smell of fresh paint escape. Even the room occupied by Ro and Nuri in the motel had been redecorated. More significantly, the wreckage left behind after the attack was being bulldozed away to make way for new workshops and businesses. Each evening, the truck stop filled with lorries whose drivers dined in the *Mattam Janna*, which meant 'Paradise Restaurant'. Ro and Nuri ate there whenever they could. It felt like home to them. Mehmet, the proprietor, was in his element meeting the needs of dozens of hungry drivers. Young Amoun was there too, with Aysha and baby Azhar. Amoun had turned out to be a gifted chef, and Mehmet taught him just about everything he could think of. Aysha's talents lay in the little office next to the kitchen. Her shrewd balancing of food stocks and budget had helped to set the dining room back on its feet. Mehmet noted her business acumen, handed her responsibilities commensurate with her abilities and rewarded her appropriately.

Ro and Nuri were still enjoying the novelty of being employees instead of scraping a living from their own endeavours. Like Amoun, Nuri had discovered talents hitherto unknown. He took to the office computer like a camel to sand. It was becoming apparent that Nuri's abilities would be wasted on merely 'running'. Ro found himself happy to pursue a variety of practical tasks in the new premises. Sometimes he worked in the warehouse loading trailers. At other times he would be sent to assist in the workshop. Finally, he settled for working with the shunters.

Rather as Rashid had predicted, the elderly Mercedes tractor units made redundant by the acquisition of Kamyonistan-TIR were decommissioned, repainted and retired as yard shunters. The Iranian drivers, having become somewhat circumspect as a result of Rashid's narrow escape in Turkey, were only too pleased to man these vehicles. Their duties ranged from moving trailers around in the yard, to retrieving loaded trailers from various factories and businesses in the transport zone. Rashid took Ro under his wing and gave him a thorough grounding in the art of manoeuvring articulated lorries in tight spaces.

One humid, overcast morning, Rashid was asked to take one of the more respectable looking shunters with an empty trailer to meet a lorry parked in a services area on the outskirts of Damascus. Because part of the visiting lorry's load needed to be transhipped to the empty trailer, he took Ro too. Nuri happened to be at a loose end and he joined them.

The traffic was heavy as they chugged into Damascus. A big, four-wheeled cart, pulled by two long-eared donkeys, made its way in the opposite direction against the flow of traffic. It was driven by two little boys aged seven and eight, who were oblivious to what was going on around them and who were gesticulating at one another in animated conversation. 'You can't walk on a cloud, it's impossible,' said one.

'Well, a mouse could,' said the other.

'No, he'd fall through the clouds.'

'What about an ant, then?' the younger boy asked.

'That's different. I think an ant could.'

'Is that where ants come from, then – the clouds?'

'Course not!'

'Why not?'

'Because that's paradise: on the clouds. You couldn't have ants in paradise, silly!'

'Why not?'

'Because they'd bite everyone… angels and that.'

'What angels?'

'Don't you know anything? They're like people but made out of clouds.'

'Will we go to paradise, then?' the younger one asked.

'Dunno yet. Only if we turn out to be good Muslims.' Cars surged round the cart, horns blaring. The older boy yanked on the reins and steered his equipage into a roadside coach park and services area. Rashid turned into its other entrance and parked alongside the lorry that they had arranged to meet.

While the two truck drivers swapped tales of the traffic, Ro and Nuri slipped off for a quick wander round. Behind the coach parking area, they were astonished to find a man with two impeccably groomed camels. They approached the keeper and greeted him. 'They're for tourists,' he told them, in answer to their questions. 'Coaches stop here on their way to and from Damascus. The tourists like to take pictures, or ride a few steps.'

'Were they expensive?' Nuri asked.

'No; a man gave me twenty camels for my wife,' the man joked.

'How much do you want for them?' Ro asked, impetuously.

'Ten wives apiece,' came the reply.

Ro turned to Nuri and said, 'Got any wives on you, mate?'

'No, they're in my other trousers,' said Nuri.

'But...' Ro began, but he was laughing too much to carry on.

'The camels are very beautiful,' Nuri sighed.

'Ideal for truck washing with,' Ro prompted.

'Perfect,' Nuri murmured.

'But think of winter, when the water freezes on your hands. This winter you'll be working with your computer in a nice, warm office,' Ro said.

'You wouldn't know what to do with one of these things,' the man said. 'You have to grow up with them to understand them.'

'I daresay,' Nuri replied, glancing at the man's big stick. Nuri had never carried a stick while driving camels. A blast from Rashid's horn summoned them and they bade the cameleer farewell.

Raindrops began to fall out of the sky as they crossed the coach park. They were nearly run over by the donkey cart, its drivers having collected useful rubbish from the bins. 'Watch where you're going!' Ro shouted.

'We don't have to,' one grubby boy shouted back gleefully. He was standing on the driving bench holding the reins.

'Why not?' shouted Ro.

'We're going to paradise!' Both boys danced with their arms and grinned happily.

'You're already there, little ones,' Ro said. 'Make the most of it while you can!'

'I think that's what Bingo would have said,' Nuri smiled, when the cart had passed.

It was raining heavily by the time they reached the lorries. All four of them crushed into the hot cab of the Merc. 'We'll sit it out and see what the weather does,' Rashid suggested, lighting up two cigarettes. 'What's that smell?'

'Camel shit,' Nuri said nonchalantly, examining his sandals.

When the rain dwindled to drizzle, the drivers and Ro set to transhipping cartons of mineral water from one trailer to the other. Nuri was unable to assist, so he went to have another look at the camels. It was hot work on the trailers, for the rain had done little to diminish the mugginess of the weather. Rashid reproached himself for failing to bring a sheet in anticipation of the downpour. Fifteen minutes later, a shout drew their attention. From round the front of the nearest coach, appeared a figure on a galloping camel. It was Nuri. His face was alight and his demeanour triumphant. He pulled up alongside the trailer, breathless with excitement. Behind him the man came running and waving his stick. Nuri was laughing.

'You didn't tell me you could ride a camel!' the man yelled crossly.

'You didn't ask,' Nuri said. 'When you refused to let me sit on the camel, you made two assumptions: firstly, that I couldn't ride a camel with only one arm; and secondly, that even with two arms I couldn't!'

'All right, you've made your point,' the cameleer muttered.

'I am of the Bedu,' Nuri said grandly. 'I grew up with camels from infancy.' By now, Ro and the drivers were holding their sides. In the end, even the camel driver saw the funny side of their altercation.

As the old Merc puffed and panted up the mountain road from Damascus, Rashid pointed out the first diggings of a new access road running south from Kamyonistan to the main Homs–Damascus road. Some of the ground surface had been scraped away, and the landscape was dotted with yellow construction machines. Rashid drove into the old access road to the north of the transport zone and pulled over. He got out so that Ro could drive the final couple of kilometres into Kamyonistan. Two years previously, his uncle had taught him to drive the ERF on this road. Now, Ro was making rapid progress at the wheel, though he was still officially underage for the job.

'Let's go and get some grub at the Janna first,' Nuri suggested. Rashid agreed and Ro engaged a low gear to swing into the TIR parking through the great Islamic gateway with its twin minarets. To their surprise, the compound was full of diggers, levellers, rollers, tippers and a tar-laying machine. Ro parked and the three headed for the restaurant. The tables inside were filled with construction workers drinking *shay* and smoking.

'What's happening here, then?' Rashid asked Mehmet, when they had ordered.

'Haven't you heard? The parking compound is going to be surfaced at long last!'

'It'll be chaos here,' Rashid complained.

'But imagine Kamyonistan without dust!' exclaimed Mehmet. 'It'll be paradise!'

'The Janna will live up to its name for once,' Nuri put in.

'It'll be brilliant in winter,' Ro said feelingly. 'Just think of all the mud that won't get walked into this place.' Oddly, the thought crossed his mind that without dust and mud, it would not feel like Kamyonistan any more.

'Ho-ho, me hearties! What's going on here then?' a voice bellowed from the entrance. Framed in the doorway, they could see the portly form of Jumbo, a jolly, bearded English driver and a regular in Kamyonistan. Ro and Nuri welcomed him. Introductions were made. There was much news to exchange.

'Ro can drive a lorry,' Nuri said.

'Nuri can drive a computer,' Ro said.

'And a camel!' added Rashid and he told Jumbo about their exploits in the outskirts of the capital.

'Eric's on his way down with a "seller" and I believe Bingo is somewhere in the pipeline,' Jumbo told them. 'There's been no Middle-East work for weeks.' They drank *shay* at the counter, then, while Rashid took the lorry round to the yard, Jumbo and the lads adjourned to a table on the veranda and dined overlooking the TIR parking as the sun went down.

Gateway to the Orient

Three days later, Eric, the driver and journalist, sat in a garden chair in front of his 'seller' – a Roadhaus-cabbed MAN with a flatbed trailer carrying crated machinery. He was stripped to the waist and he sat with his hands behind his head and his legs splayed out in front of him. 'I still can't believe you've done that, mate,' he said to Jumbo, nodding at Jumbo's wagon. The gleaming white Volvo FH16 stood before them. Attached to it was Jumbo's garment trailer, now painted in yellow with KAMYONISTAN LONG-HAUL SERVICES stencilled along each side in both English and Arabic.

'They seem a very competent outfit,' Jumbo said. 'I spent two days ducking in and out of their office. Anyway, the paint job's free.'

'They'll do their fruit in England when you pull up outside the freight forwarder's office with that,' Eric said.

'Keep 'em on their toes then, won't it!' Jumbo chuckled.

'I hope so, for your sake.'

'Don't be such a stick-in-the-mud!' Jumbo said. 'I thought you were a fan of Kamyonistan.'

'Well, yes. It's certainly encouraging to see how it has been reorientated in the past few months.'

'How do you mean?' Ro asked. 'Reorientated from what to what by what?' He had just joined them, after slipping away on an open-ended errand.

'Well, look how the rocket attack has given the place a new sense of self-respect,' Eric said.

'OK. Physically, it's being reorientated from the mountains towards Damascus by the new access road,' Ro said.

'Precisely,' Eric said. 'At a commercial level, the business community of Kamyonistan's collective sense of purpose is being reorientated from the arena of international conflict towards future prosperity, by its positive resolve.'

'Shit! I'd never thought of that,' Ro said.

'Can't see the wood for the trees, then!' Eric grinned.

'I get it,' Ro said. 'So at another level, Kamyonistan's existence as a construct in the minds of the Paradise Club is being reorientated from chaos towards paradise by their optimistic outlook.'

'Smart-arsed little bastard!' Jumbo laughed. 'You're wasted as a shunter.'

'Not at all! This is a man who understands Greater Kamyonistan,' said Eric. 'Happy shunters make the world go round.'

'There's a song there, somewhere,' said Jumbo. 'And it's all very well to talk of prosperity, but haven't you noticed that Middle-East food prices are escalating at an alarming rate? Talking of which, are we going to have a bit of lunch before I go off and load?'

'This is your last chance to do that,' Ro advised. 'Tomorrow, if the moon is right, Ramadan starts, so the restaurant won't be serving during the day.'

'Oh no!' Eric said. 'This is the worst time of the year to have Ramadan. It's too hot and the days are too long. Fifteen hours without food and drink is a long time.'

'My kidneys wouldn't put up with it,' Jumbo said. 'I gave up trying years ago.'

'Well, as a Muslim – even if I'm not a very good one – I'll be expected to abstain. I'm not looking forward to it,' Ro said.

They sat and gazed out at the parked lorries and the heavy plant that was scattered among them. 'I wonder why the contractors haven't started surfacing this lot,' Jumbo said, getting up. He locked his cab and admired the new paintwork on his trailer. 'Who's a pretty boy, then?' he chirruped, half to himself.

They made for the Janna. It was full of contractors. 'Haven't these people got anything to do?' Eric asked Mehmet.

'No. They're ready for work, but the money hasn't been put up. It'll be murder tomorrow, with a lot of dissatisfied workers made bad-tempered by Ramadan,' Mehmet grumbled.

The three of them had a snack and a drink. Jumbo wanted beer, but Aysha had already taken it off the shelves in preparation for Ramadan, so he settled for *shay* instead. Eric was just asking Jumbo where he was loading for, when a stocky man in a shabby sports jacket jumped onto a table and began shouting out an announcement of some kind in Arabic. A terrific roar of protest went up. Workmen slammed their glasses down and made for the door. There was anger in their voices as they left. Outside, engines could be heard starting up. Mehmet stood and watched the dust billow and swirl around the truck stop. 'We'll have our dust for a long time yet, I'm afraid,' he said, sadly.

'Why, what's up?' Eric asked.

'Corruption,' Mehmet said, shaking his head. 'The money that was allocated for resurfacing this compound has been siphoned off into the pocket of some heartless swine driving a black BMW. It happens all the time, I'm afraid.'

'Isn't there a law against it?'

'Yes, but there's corruption in the police, the legal service, the justice system and everywhere. Corruption's the bane of the Middle East.'

'And Russia,' Jumbo added consolingly.

'And Africa,' Ro contributed.

'And Italy,' Eric added.

'Not to mention Belgium,' Jumbo laughed.

'Then there's Essex,' Eric said, darkly.

Ro walked back to the KLHS yard. The workshop was deserted, so he popped his head round the door of the shunters' rest room. It was full of cigarette smoke and cheerful shouting. They were playing cards. The driver's door of Rashid's usual unit was open so Ro looked inside. Rashid was distressed. He sensed Ro's weight upon the step as the cab dipped slightly. Quickly drying his face, he put on a jolly expression but Ro was having none of it.

'Are you homesick?' Ro asked, directly.

'Yes,' Rashid said, miserably. 'I'm depressed, too.'

'Why?'

'I don't really know. I've always suffered from it. The trouble is, homesickness and depression have the same feeling, so I can't be sure which I'm suffering from,' Rashid said.

'Is it bad?'

'Sometimes it's very bad.'

'Too bad to ignore?'

'Yes. I feel as if I am standing in front of a brick wall and that's it. I can't move a brick wall! I can't go round a brick wall. It just blocks my way so I'm stuck and I can't go forwards.'

'Like a prison,' Ro said.

'Worse! There's no parole, no remission, no escape and no release.'

'I'll put the kettle on,' Ro said, pulling the stove and glasses out of the locker.

'Up against a damned brick wall!' Rashid muttered, distantly.

Ro paused, then turned to Rashid. 'Break the wall down,' he said.

'I can't.'

'Imagine it. Do it in your head.'

'If I visualise bashing it down, I would have to pretend to be Superman. How can I believe in that?'

'Don't be someone else. Be yourself. Take out one single brick. Then pull out another one, and another. You can destroy that wall in your head.'

'I'll do that now, Ro. Forget the *shay*. Go and help your friend Nuri, or something. I'll have to do this on my own, in peace. Thank you, son. Thank you.'

That afternoon, Eric left for Saudi to tip his load of machinery and to run empty into Qatar to sell his truck. Jumbo loaded a mixture of boxed workwear and hanging shirts in his resplendent trailer, taking extra care to guard against stowaways. Even though the supply of potential stowaways appeared to have dried up for the present, it did not mean that there were none in Kamyonistan.

In the freight agency office, Nuri was joined by eighteen-year-old Kamal, an affable young Syrian from Damascus, who arrived in the bus that brought in clothes factory workers. Kamal confided to Nuri that he was saving up for a motorbike with which to perform his tasks as a runner. His brief was to cover the outlying parts of the transport zone, whereas Nuri's patch was the yard and the truck stop across the road. Kamal and Nuri hit it off from the outset. Perceiving that Nuri's spoken English was far more advanced than his written English, Kamal helped Nuri to decipher computer messages with a patience and sensitivity that ensured that Nuri's self-esteem remained intact throughout their exchanges.

During the final week of preparations for the belated official relocation of Kamyonistan Long-Haul Services to its new premises, Ro was deployed to assist Nuri, Kamal and ancillary staff with the removal of office contents from the freight agency building by the truck stop. The furniture, filing cabinets and fittings were moved with little trouble. It was the files, records and computer equipment that caused the problems. The office manager, Maryam, was highly organised, however, and she was able to direct everything to its proper place with the minimum of fuss.

The great day arrived. Six tilt trailers, formerly the property of Kamyonistan-TIR, had been refurbished and now sported yellow canopies and violet side boards in full KLHS livery. Rashid parked these to form a large, awning-covered square in which the official opening was to take place. Beyond the tilts, in the parking area, a dozen KLHS subcontractors parked their trucks; this being their new operating base. Chairs were out, boxes of geraniums lined the resplendent tilts and a microphone stood at the front.

During the speeches, a number of introductions were made. The Owner gave the impression that he was the head of a happy family. Ro had no idea that the company he worked for employed so many people. After introducing the Director, Mustafa, the Owner sat down and beamed expectantly. Mustafa did not disappoint. He delivered a speech filled with amusing rhetoric and then introduced Maryam, the Office Manager, with whom the boys had already made an acquaintance. She introduced the office clerks, before inviting Ahmad, the Personnel Manager, to join her. Ro and Nuri knew Ahmad too, for he had recruited them in the first place. The Freight Agent then stood up and introduced his runners, Nuri and Kamal. Next, the Warehouse Manager introduced his warehousemen, forklift drivers and loaders. After that, the Container Supervisor was called upon to introduce his top-loader driver and gantry crane operators. Fahmy, formerly the jovial Transport Manager for Kamyonistan-TIR, was introduced in his new role as Traffic Manager. Rashid then brought on his team of shunters and the assistant shunter, Ro. The Workshop Manager, Mohammed, warmly commended his maintenance team to the audience, followed by the kitchen staff and the Estate Manager, who introduced a team of cleaners and caretakers. Finally, a Syrian representative of the army of lorry drivers who subcontracted for KLHS introduced his colleagues in absentia. The whole occasion was wound up by a brief message of goodwill from the chairman of Kamyonistan's chamber of commerce. Refreshments were fondly imagined being served, it being Ramadan.

'Are you coming to the Janna tonight?' Ro asked Nuri and Kamal. 'There's a band coming, and I'm hoping it'll be those musicians we had during the attack.'

'I have to go back to Damascus,' Kamal said. 'When I get my motorbike, it'll be different.' He turned to Nuri and said, 'Then I'll be able to whisk you off to Damascus and go clubbing!'

'Why don't you stay with us tonight? It's the weekend so you don't have to worry about work,' Nuri suggested. Ro hesitated. He liked Kamal but he felt uneasy about the way that Kamal bonded so easily with Nuri. Berating himself for silly jealousy, he shook his fears off and prepared himself for the evening.

Ro's hunch had been right: the group known to Jumbo as the Kamyonistan Café Band provided the entertainment. In reality it was called something else, of course. That night Kamal slept on their settee.

Ramadan

Sunlight dappled Titania's garden with a multitude of greens and yellows. Late summer was merging into early autumn. It was a time of year Titania had long associated with a certain crispness in the air; of new school uniforms and children returned to school, brown and relaxed after the long, hot, jolly summer hols. Now retired, her heart went out to former colleagues juggling with piles of exercise books among chattering pupils. A blackbird bounced across her lawn. Running through her mind the list of things she had planned to do that day, she reflected that she had not looked at her emails since the weekend. There was bread to buy and something to get for her evening meal. A visit to the library was long overdue, and she really needed to practise her soprano line in the choral society's forthcoming performance of that complex oratorio, *The Dream of Gerontius* by Edward Elgar. She moved to the open piano and adumbrated the line, 'Praise to the holiest' with her hand shape and with the silent 'o' of her mouth. In an instant, she had rehearsed it in her head without making a sound. Smiling, she went to her laptop in the other room and switched it on. The clatter of her letter box announced the arrival of bills. There was a time when that noise signalled the arrival of personal missives from friends who wrote letters. Now, it was her laptop that performed that function. There were three messages. One was from Ro.

<Dear Titania, I hope you are well and happy. We are doing well here. The company we work for is very friendly and there's lots of work for us to do. Nuri works mostly in the office, ferrying paperwork out to the drivers. I mostly work in the yard and the zone, driving a shunter and moving trailers about. I also have to coordinate loads and trailers and make sure that everything's in the right place at the right time. We've got a new friend from work called Kamal. He's our age and he works with Nuri.

Ramadan

It's the last week of Ramadan here now and the days seem very long without anything inside us. Sometimes I drink bottled water when no one's looking, just to protect my poor kidneys!

<By the way, we've moved. We are still in the motel, but we've moved upstairs. The manager suffers from gout and doesn't like the stairs, so he's moved out of the flat on the top floor into our little room on the ground floor. He's going to turn two ground-floor rooms into a flat for himself. I reckon he's a bit of an 'alchy' and just wants to be nearer the bar in reception. Now we live on the top floor in his old flat. It's not very big but the whole of the roof terrace belongs to it. The views up there are fantastic, so we live outside most of the time and it's lovely and private. Some nights we sleep under the stars. To the south, towards Damascus, we can look down onto the roofs of the restaurant and the drivers' suq and see the line of the new access road. To the north, are the wonderful mountains that form the backdrop to Kamyonistan. Also, we can see the main gate and the transport zone and the old access road. To the west, we can see the stump of our dear old minaret, the drivers' mosque, the fuel compound, the newly bulldozed military compounds and immediately below us the TIR park. To the east, there are more mountains and below us, across the road we can see Kamyonistan Long-Haul Services where we work. We seem to have landed firmly on our feet!

<Jumbo and Eric have been here. Jumbo has signed up with the freight forwarder and is hoping to do their work. Eric is sceptical about the regularity of payments but we'll have to see. We hope to see Bingo soon. Amoun and Aysha send their love. So does baby Azhar, I think. I couldn't get much sense out of him yesterday when I asked. If the combination of rapid leg thrusting, dribbling and intermittent smiling constitutes affirmative body language, then consider yourself a recipient of his love. Look after yourself. Lots of love, Ro and Nuri.>

Titania Roberts sighed, smiled and turned off the laptop. She would allow her reply to ease itself into her mind as the day wore on. First, she wrote a list of things to do, which helped her to avoid challenging her short-term memory. Then she went to tidy herself ready to go out. When she reached the front door, she realised that she had forgotten where she had put the list that helped her to forget forgetfulness. Irritated, she wrote another, and was so pleased that she had remembered everything from the original list that her irritation was banished.

Bingo, Middle-East driver and fully fledged member of the Kamyonistan Paradise Club, barrelled through the mist of a dual carriageway in Northern England until he came to 'the second roundabout after a red and white carpet warehouse that comes up on your left about half a mile after the fifteen-foot-high railway bridge'. If only satellite navigations would give the kind of instructions that lorry drivers give each other, Bingo thought to himself. He followed the next instruction, which he kept in his head: 'Take the second exit and turn into the first set of metal gates on your left; take it wide or your trailer wheels won't clear the fire hydrant hidden in the grass.' It was not rocket science to give sensible directions, he reflected smugly. He slammed on the brakes and the lorry shuddered to a halt. He'd been so busy watching for the fire hydrant that he nearly failed to see the telegraph pole to the right of the gateway. Why hadn't that been included in the instructions? If he steered hard right in low gear, he'd straighten up and clear both the hydrant and the pole. He accelerated into the yard and saw in front of him a big yellow trailer with 'Kamyonistan Long-Haul Services' written on the side and Jumbo's unit attached to the front of it. He could not believe his eyes. Bingo hit the air horns. He saw Jumbo's cab rock as he climbed out, slammed the door and waddled back towards Bingo.

'What's the matter with getting out of the cab and coming to talk with me properly, you uncommunicative swine!' he shouted good-naturedly. 'You're not on the motorway now; you're in a yard, mate.'

'Are you calling me an autistic bastard?' Bingo called from his seat.

'No, of course not: out of respect for my illegitimate autistic daughter,' Jumbo said.

'Have you got the kettle on?' Bingo asked, climbing down from the DAF XF.

'Yes. Come and sit in my cab. These people haven't even opened up the warehouse yet.'

'You haven't even got a daughter!' Bingo muttered.

'So what? Your description fits any daughter I might have had! But it's not very politically correct to say so, I suppose.'

'Politically correct? The worst insult you can use these days is to call someone a healthy, English, white, middle-class male and it's not even politically incorrect to say it yet! Never mind; where are you loading for – Syria?'

'No,' said Jumbo. 'Tunisia. I'm loading for Menzil Jemil and loading home from Sfax.'

'Been there before?'

'Yes, mate; I like doing Tunisia, you can park anywhere and no one bothers you.'

'Where are you shipping out from – Genoa or Marseille?'

'Dunno yet. Seen this trailer?'

'Yes. You have some explaining to do, Jumbo, my man.'

'I see you still have a yellow tilt, mate. The black letters of KLHS would look just right on yours!'

Ro was called into the traffic office at lunchtime. Fahmy shook his hand and asked if he was getting on all right and enjoying the work. Ro replied that he was and that he hoped to learn something about running repairs in the workshop at some stage. Fahmy said he would see what he could arrange. In the meantime would Ro like to go out on another trip because he had a driver in need of an assistant, that driver's own assistant having succumbed to something intestinal. 'Get your overnight gear, then. You're off to Amman, the capital of Jordan.'

Ro ran to collect his things. On the way out of the apartment, in the half-light of the stairwell, he met Nuri and a tall, dark, handsome youth whom he realised was Kamal. Later, in the yard, Ro was introduced to a Syrian driver who ran a smart Scania 144 with a fridge trailer. If they made good progress, they would just make it to Amman and back before Ramadan finished and Eid al Fitr started.

The Syrian didn't treat Ro as a dogsbody, as Ro had feared. Rather, he treated him with the kind of respect due to a guest. Ro learned much from the young driver. In Amman, they loaded with fruit and found time to eat out. The outing made a pleasant break from the yard.

Once back in Kamyonistan, Ro decided to go to bed early to catch up on lost sleep. Up on the roof terrace after the sunset call to prayer, he drank a glass of water with a lemon squeezed into it. Then, exhausted, he flung himself on the bed and slept. He awoke at eleven. It was dark. Nuri had not returned. Ro got up, put the light on and made a cup of tea. The bed was all over the place. He straightened the sheet, but it became untucked at the foot of the bed. Tucking it back into place, he found a blue sock with snowmen printed on. It did not belong to him, or to Nuri, who almost never wore socks; and if he did, he wore Ro's. He sat on the edge of the bed, stretching and relaxing the sock as if it were an accordion, trying to make sense of the object in his hands. It had ceased to become a sock and was taking on a new life as something threatening and challenging.

The kettle boiled and he got up. Making tea momentarily displaced his incipient fears. Then it hit him. He was forced to conclude that someone else had been in his bed. If someone else had been in his bed he must have been there with Nuri. If someone else had been in his bed with Nuri, it could only have been Kamal. Anger began to fester and multiply inside him. This was a new thing. It had never before occurred to him that anyone else might want to sleep with Nuri. It just had not arisen.

When Nuri came in, he exclaimed in delight, 'Ro! You're back! How did it go?' He sat on the bed with a bounce. Ro pulled the sheet round his shoulder and turned the other way.

'Leave me alone,' he said, icily.

'But Ro! What's the matter?'

Ro remained silent.

'Ro? Please tell me. What's wrong?'

Ro did not utter another word. He lay smouldering against his pillow. Should he challenge Nuri? Should he challenge Kamal? Yes, he thought, he would tell Kamal to back off.

He woke again at two. If they had been married, Ro reflected, fidelity would have been built into the contract. The expectation of fidelity would have been voiced, and promises made. The trouble with those religious and secular regimes that outlawed same-sex marriages was that formal safeguards against infidelity were not possible. This was probably deliberate, of course, he thought bitterly, in order to make life impossible for those who would attempt such marriages. The notion that a strong enough relationship might transcend the need for safeguards strayed into his consciousness and became elusive again. To be fair, he decided, he would have run a mile from any kind of marriage to anyone.

In the morning he refused to speak to Nuri, who remained bewildered. Ro went to the yard and reported for duty. He was told to go home. Ramadan had finished; it was time to celebrate. Ro marched round to the freight office to give Kamal a piece of his mind. He might even thump him one, he didn't know yet. He found Nuri instead. The office was shut.

'Why won't you talk to me, Ro? I've never seen you like this before. Did something happen to you in Amman? Please, Ro,' Nuri pleaded.

'Don't play the innocent with me, you two-faced git!' Ro shouted.

Nuri looked horrified. 'What do you mean?'

'Kamal, of course! You've been sleeping with Kamal. Why couldn't you just tell me?'

'But I haven't, Ro. I don't think Kamal would want to sleep with me. He never stops talking about the girls in Damascus.'

'I don't believe you!'

The breaking of the great fast of Ramadan was celebrated that night in the Janna. Mehmet had persuaded the café band to return. By mid-evening the drivers of all nations were gathered happily in the smoky room, shouting at each other over the din. Ro and Nuri were both there but at opposite ends of the room. Nuri found the Jordanian driver, Wahid, who had smuggled them out of Egypt the previous year. He wanted to take him to see Ro but he did not dare. Under the watchful eyes of Amoun and Mehmet, Aysha performed a belly dance on one of the tables. Her young body drew too much attention, however, so she was quickly withdrawn. The band struck up again and Mahmout, who ran the truck wash, leapt onto the table. He strode seductively down the row of tables, his arms flowing in a mock belly-dance style. Then he lifted the hem of his jalabiya and everyone clapped and roared. He even did the faces. Ro was quite amused; he had never seen this side of Mahmout before. It was often said, especially by Bingo, that Mahmout had hidden talents. Swirling the jalabiya before him, Mahmout advanced towards Ro. Ro squirmed and retreated. Mahmout's brown legs jutted out of his odd socks and Ro, who had always nursed a dormant desire for him, suddenly thought of the possibility of a liaison. What better way to show his disapproval? He glanced at the sturdy knees and ran his eyes back down to the feet, where he noticed that one sock was red and the other was blue with little snowmen printed on it.

'It's you, you bastard!' he blazed suddenly and launched himself at Mahmout's legs, pulling him off the table. The pair rolled about on the floor in combat; then Mahmout, who was much more powerful than Ro, pinned his arms back and slammed him against the wall. Mehmet and a couple of regular drivers ushered them outside. Nuri followed.

A cool breeze blew onto the veranda. Ro's tears of rage distorted his speech. 'You've been sleeping with Nuri!' he said accusingly.

'I haven't!' Mahmout said defiantly. Then catching sight of Nuri, he added, 'Have I, Nuri?'

'Absolutely not,' Nuri said.

'*Liars! Liars!*' Ro shouted. Dramatically, he pulled out the other sock from his pocket. 'If you didn't, then how come I found this sock at the bottom of our bed, clever clogs? It's your sock, Mahmout! The other one is on your foot.' Ro pointed at the offending foot.

'I wondered where that had got to!' Mahmout said. 'Go and get Amoun, Mehmet; he can shed a light on this.'

'Tell Ro what we did the night before last, will you?' Mahmout demanded, when Amoun appeared.

'Well...' Amoun began. He looked bewildered. 'Well, Kamal, Mahmout here, Nuri and I had our meals bagged up so that we could take them up to your apartment and eat them on the terrace. Then it got chilly and we went inside. We played cards on the bed for hours and talked and talked until nearly dawn... Why?

What's the matter? Oh, I see someone's found your sock at last! We spent ages looking for that.'

'I'm sorry,' Ro said. He shook Mahmout's hand. 'I'm really sorry.' He walked round the tables and faced Nuri. 'I should have trusted you. I wish I had trusted you,' he said to Nuri.

'Trust is one of the most important parts of love,' Nuri said. 'If you had trusted me, you would have told me what was upsetting you, instead of coming here fighting like an English football hooligan.' Ro hugged him and said he was sorry.

'Let's go home,' Nuri said.

In the dark they strolled slowly. 'What must you think of me?' Ro said. 'How could I be such a fool, to jump at shadows like that? What are you going to do with me?'

'Forgive you, of course. That's an important part of love too,' Nuri said. He turned away, his shoulders heaving. Ro thought he was crying, but when Nuri turned back his eyes were alight and he was laughing. 'When you pulled him off the table, swearing and rolling on the floor, you thought you were the last of the hard bastards, didn't you!'

Then Ro began to laugh as well. Nuri took his hand. All was well in their world.

Greater Kamyonistan

As echoes of the afternoon call to prayer faded from the little walled garden behind the drivers' mosque, Ro and Nuri sat on a low bench next to the fountain. The fountain had not worked again since the attack on Kamyonistan, but the palm trees and spilling bougainvillea thrived. Doves warbled in the oleander.

'Was Bingo right about Greater Kamyonistan?' Nuri asked.

'What do you mean?' Ro said.

'He said that Greater Kamyonistan was that other country now,' said Nuri. 'He was sort of joking, but he was still creating a new idea.'

'That's the Kamyonistan paradigm in our heads, isn't it? The paradise location in our minds.'

'Yes, I understand about that,' Nuri said. 'But Bingo always said that paradise was in childhood, and that if we get it right, we can take it with us through life by hanging on to our child selves.'

'So?'

'So, how can paradise be located in childhood and Greater Kamyonistan at the same time? How can those two different sorts of place be that other country?'

'Ah, I see,' Ro said. 'Perhaps he meant that paradise means different things to different people. To some it means childhood and to others it means Greater Kamyonistan.'

'I don't think so. I think he meant that there is a definite relationship between the two,' Nuri persisted.

'Perhaps, then, he meant that Greater Kamyonistan is a useful vehicle for sustaining the childhood self during adulthood,' Ro offered.

'That would make sense,' said Nuri. 'There is a recognisable relationship there.'

'We'll have to ask him when he comes,' Ro murmured.

He paused to listen to the distant hum of the world beyond

the stone walls of their secret garden at the heart of Kamyonistan. They heard a lorry make its way out of the compound and up the access road. It was either low-powered or overloaded, Ro thought, as it laboured sequentially through the gears. A cock crowed behind the restaurant. Nuri shuffled and scratched his head. 'Do you remember that meeting, when we first had the Paradise Club?' he said.

'Of course! Uncle Norman and Kees were there,' Ro answered.

'Well, do you remember what Eric said about truck stops?'

'Vaguely.'

'Well I've heard him talk about it since then, in the Janna,' Nuri said. 'He argued that a fragment of paradise lies at the interface of a trucker's journey and his resting place, the truck stop.'

'Yes, I do remember now,' Ro said. 'What made you think of that?'

'Well, perhaps the relationship between Greater Kamyonistan and childhood is similar,' Nuri said. Ro sat up.

'Yes?'

'Perhaps a form of paradise lies at the interface of the child self's journey and Greater Kamyonistan,' Nuri suggested.

'Oh yes!' Ro said. He smiled. 'Oh yes! That's true for you and for me because our rite of passage took us from childhood into Greater Kamyonistan.'

'It's also true for Bingo, who had a second crack at his rite of passage and ended up in Greater Kamyonistan,' Nuri said.

'So using Eric's model, Kamyonistan represents the stopping place and the rite of passage represents the journey.'

'Exactly.'

'I might have to tickle you,' Ro replied.

'No, wait,' said Nuri, staving him off with his arm. 'Remember when we tried doing meditation that time in England?'

'Yes?'

'That safe little place deep inside us that we go to when we meditate: it's the same place, isn't it?' Nuri asked, and the question hung in the air along with the cooing of the doves.

'Yes,' Ro replied at length. 'Yes, I think it is. Once you know that enchanted place inside you, it can become a secret garden, a truck stop or anything you want, I suppose. I'll email Titania again tonight and see what she thinks.'

The next three days were hectic. KLHS's big yard filled up with yellow and white lorries belonging to subbies from all over the Middle East. There were even some from Eastern Europe. Nuri was rushed off his feet, matching correct paperwork with loads and in turn matching those with trailers. Ro shunted more trailers than he'd ever done, working a nineteen-hour shift on the third day. They were exhausted. KLHS's acquisition of the container terminal was resulting in the company's evolution from 'freight forwarder' to 'freight forwarder with transport hub'. The lorries just kept on coming.

<Dear Ro and Nuri,> Titania emailed. <Thank you for your thoughtful and thought-provoking message. I do believe you are right. I've been meditating for many years now and I can see no fault with your argument that our notion of Greater Kamyonistan could double as that enchanted place within us if we chose. It gets complicated when you start cross-referencing that with the child self, and more so if you factor in the transition of child self to adulthood; but I can see how Eric's model can be used. I'd be interested to hear what Bingo himself thinks.

<In the meantime, I've been racking my brains for some equivalent to Greater Kamyonistan in literature, but it isn't easy. The only thing I can come up with is Tolkien's Rivendell, which not only shares with Greater Kamyonistan its sense of security and euphoria but also its very raison d'être as a stopping place. I wonder how Tolkien addicts would view the prospect of a Seddon-Atkinson and tilt parked outside the 'last homely house'. Legolas would do his nut! The Quest for Greater Kamyonistan continues. Anyway, must fly now: we've got to rehearse the Elgar for next weekend. Don't work too hard! Take care, Titania.>

The veranda at the Janna was bathed in sunlight. Amoun squinted at the shimmering lorries in the TIR park. He lit a cigarette and offered one to Ro, who shook his head mechanically. A good deal of noise issued from the dining area where something had ignited laughter. Mehmet rushed out onto the veranda holding Azhar's carrycot. Aysha and Nuri crowded behind him. 'Azhar's laid an egg!' Aysha announced, delightedly.

'Well, tell him to stop laying eggs,' Amoun retorted, dryly. 'We'll only have to feed whatever hatches, and we have enough mouths to feed as it is!'

'Show me,' said Ro. He looked into the cot. Next to the baby was a brown egg. Ro giggled. 'How did that happen?'

'It may or may not have rolled off the table into his cot, but one way or another baby Azhar has seemingly laid an egg!' Mehmet laughed. A Bulgarian driver, witnessing this, reached into the pram and, with flourish, reproduced the egg from behind Aysha's ear. Clearly, it was going to be one of those mornings. A tall driver in his sixties mounted the veranda steps and strode into the domestic chaos.

'Look, Bingo: Azhar's laying eggs!' Nuri greeted him.

'I hope they're golden ones then,' Bingo replied, embracing him. 'You all look busy here. Does this mean that *shay*'s on the way?'

'And chicken kebab too, if you want,' Mehmet replied, leaning across the table to shake Bingo's hand.

'How's the DAF?' Ro asked.

'DAF's fine. Do you want to know how I am?' Bingo laughed.

'How do you do?' Ro cooed.

'A bit rough; nothing that a good dose of retirement wouldn't cure,' Bingo said, picking up little Azhar and drying his tears. 'Ciao, baby! Nice to see you in such good spirits!'

'You'd howl like that if you'd just laid an egg this size,' Nuri chuckled.

The following evening, Bingo went to meet the lads at the Janna after work, as planned. He deliberately parked close to the front of the restaurant and sat on the veranda with a beer. Nuri arrived first with Kamal, who was only stopping for a soft drink before going to Damascus. Then Ro arrived driving a shunter, which he parked ostentatiously right next to the veranda. Bingo ribbed him mercilessly for this. Sipping *shay* happily as the evening call to prayer filled the warm air, Ro's eyes alighted on

Greater Kamyonistan

Bingo's wagon. 'So am I the only little show-off to park too close to the Janna, then?' he asked mischievously.

'What do you mean?' Bingo said.

'You wouldn't be parking closer than usual so we can see what's written on the side of your tilt, by any chance?' Ro said.

'All right, touché!' Bingo laughed.

'Are you a subbie now?'

'Yes and no: I haven't signed up like Jumbo has, but I've done a deal with them. I'll do some of their Syria–UK work when the price is right, and I don't mind having their name on my tilt as it happens to be already yellow. But I draw the line at repainting the unit; head above the parapet and all that.'

'Do you think Jumbo's made a mistake, then?' Ro asked.

'Not necessarily: there's plenty of work for him, and if they pay him regularly and on time, he'll have landed on his feet. When you run one lorry, good cash flow is everything. They only need to mess him about for a couple of months and he could find himself in difficulties.'

Kamal said his goodbyes and left. The food came and Nuri raised his glass. 'To Greater Kamyonistan!' he said.

'Ah yes! Greater Kamyonistan,' Bingo mused. 'It's a sort of safer version of the real one, isn't it. What do you think?'

'We think that it's a fragment of paradise that lies at the interface of the journey from childhood to adulthood and the truck stop in which that occurs,' Ro said.

'And that as long as the child self continues with his journey through adulthood, there will always be opportunities for further glimpses of Greater Kamyonistan,' Nuri added.

'Especially when we locate Greater Kamyonistan in that enchanted place within us, where we take refuge from the world during meditation,' Ro concluded.

'Bloody hell!' said Bingo. 'I'd never thought of using the enchanted place. It fits, of course. I haven't meditated for ages, but I recognise what you mean. Mine's a wonderful place: even God can't get me there!'

'Who's protecting you, then?' Nuri asked. 'That special place is protected by God.'

'Mine isn't,' Bingo said. 'I protect it myself. 'I'm in the driving seat, so it's my responsibility to do the protecting.'

'If you are in the driving seat, what about your insurance? Isn't God your insurance certificate?' Nuri challenged.

'No. I pay and instruct the insurance man so it is still my responsibility. It's still me who initiates the protection.'

'And how do you protect your inner domain?'

'By not recognising any form of attack upon it. There is no adversary. The place is entirely safe and it always will be,' Bingo said.

'But you recognise attack in the real world,' said Ro. 'You've said so before.'

'I know, but where it matters nothing can get you,' Bingo answered.

'What about dark forces?' Ro asked.

'The only one who can poison my inner place with dark forces is me,' Bingo insisted.

'And if you do poison it because you are only human, who guides you away from destruction?' Ro wanted to know.

'*Me*. Because I know it's all down to me, I don't wreck the place hoping that someone else like God'll bail me out. I take full responsibility for the welfare of my place and moreover I hold myself responsible for it,' Bingo replied, adding, 'But don't let me put you off using God if it helps you.'

They finished their meals and watched the moon glinting from the cabs of parked trucks. Bingo thought about the boys' analysis of Greater Kamyonistan. Then he asked them, 'What do you visualise when you go into Greater Kamyonistan in your heads? I mean, what mental picture of it do you conjure up?'

'The garden,' Nuri said straight away.

'Garden? What garden?'

'Oh, just a garden in Kamyonistan,' Nuri said vaguely as he caught Ro's eye.

'And what about you, Ro?' asked Bingo.

'Well...' Ro wanted to nominate the mosque garden too, but it was his and Nuri's special place; about the only one left, now that the ERF had gone, and their minaret too. 'Perhaps that little corner of the compound where our lorry and minaret used to be,' he said. The more he thought about it, the more he liked the idea.

'What about you, Bingo?' Nuri asked.

'The lorry,' Bingo replied. 'I think I'll visualise the bunk of my cosy cab standing out there in the midst of it all. That would take no effort at all.'

'I like it!' Ro grinned. 'Perhaps I'll try the same with the shunter.'

'I wonder where Titania would choose,' Bingo said. 'Somewhere in the suq, probably; she loves it in there!'

'Or the Janna,' Ro suggested.

Nuri thought about the garden and wondered what it would be like in the moonlight. They'd never been there at night. He brushed Ro's hand with his. Ro started, then got up and stretched. 'Come on, Nuri, we've got work tomorrow,' he said.

Bingo went inside for a nightcap and Nuri steered Ro out into the TIR parking. 'Where are we going, Nuri?'

'You'll see.'

The garden was eerie, but familiar. Moonlight had drained it of colour. It reminded Ro a little of the day of the rocket attack when they had stood under the dust-coated palms and shrubs. They sat on the bench and Ro held Nuri close. He wondered if Nuri visualised the garden with both of them in it or not, but he did not dare ask him. Nuri snuggled his head against Ro's and slipped his hand into Ro's hands. The thing about moments like these, he thought, was that you didn't have to go into that special place inside you because you were already there inside it.

Compound Nouns

Ro, Nuri and Kamal sat cheek by jowl in the shunter, munching chicken wraps outside the restaurant. Both doors were open but Ro had left the engine running because the battery was 'tired with a capital F', as he had put it. Diesel exhaust stung their eyes. 'The TIR parki looks quiet today,' Ro said.

'Parki?' Nuri questioned.

'Well, that's what the Turks write, isn't it?' Ro said, scornfully.

'There's no dot on the "I" at the end of TIR parki in Turkish,' Kamal said. 'You have to say "TIR parkuh" instead.'

'Why can't they just write TIR park?' Ro asked.

'Because the "uh" on the end denotes a compound noun,' said Kamal. 'The word "park" on its own doesn't have an "uh", but combined with another noun it acquires the suffix "uh".'

'A compound noun? That's a very apposite sort of a noun to be naming a parking compound! But isn't "TIR" an adjective in that context?' Ro said.

'No: a TIR is an international lorry in Turkish, rather than an international convention,' Kamal replied.

'It must mean both to a *gumruk* official,' said Ro, referring to customs personnel.

'That's true. But listen, Ro, never mind the finer points of your Turkish; we've got to get your Arabic sorted out. You speak half Egyptian Arabic and half Syrian Arabic, and your reading and writing of Arabic is atrocious, if I may say so.'

'I'll pick it up,' Ro said dismissively.

'You won't, you need lessons,' Kamal said.

'He's right,' Nuri sighed. 'My English is exactly the same. I can speak it fluently but I read and write it like a child.'

'I'll teach you,' Kamal said. 'Let me stay at your place for a while and I'll teach you to read and write properly. We'll get you conjugating some of these verbs properly too. You should correct him more, Nuri! Hey, look at the time; we'd better get back to the office.'

'We'll pick up the trailer I need on the way,' Ro said, putting the unit into gear and releasing the handbrake.

Slowly, the old unit bounced and rolled across the dusty compound. Ro drove along the rows of parked lorries, seeking the loaded trailer he had come to collect. Eventually, he espied it in their old corner under the palm tree. Wedged into that now broken corner, where the ERF had once stood between the palm and the minaret, they noticed two Portakabins, resembling shipping containers with windows, stacked one upon the other. A stovepipe protruded from the roof and an outside stairway slanted across the front. Upon closer inspection, they noticed men wearing *shamaghs* sorting out the heaped stones of the destroyed minaret. While Ro backed onto the trailer and connected the air lines and electrics, Nuri and Kamal quizzed the workmen.

They returned to the cab and Ro pulled out of the slot with a stream of grey diesel exhaust. The trailer was heavy and the lorry crawled back towards the grand entrance. 'They are restoring our minaret, *il-hamdulilah*!' Nuri exclaimed.

'Great news!' replied Ro. 'I bet they won't give us the key.'

'I hadn't thought of that,' Nuri said.

'Who's doing it, and why?' Ro asked.

'The foreman told us they had been commissioned by the original architects who designed the truck stop,' Kamal said.

'Well, let's hope the funds for it don't go the same way as the funds for resurfacing the TIR park,' Ro said.

'The TIR compound noun?' giggled Nuri.

'That and all,' Ro chuckled. Kamal looked perplexed. If he was going to move in with these two, he would have to get used to their strange sense of humour, he thought. So did Ro and Nuri.

A fortnight later, Ro had just picked up Nuri and Kamal for lunch in the Janna, when he noticed a British-registered lorry in the TIR park. It was a yellow garment trailer in KLHS livery identical to Jumbo's, headed by a white Scania 144 bristling with spotlamps and sporting a camel bar. Ro pulled alongside it and was astonished to find Eric cleaning the windscreen. 'Eric!' he called from the driver's seat. Searching his mind for what Jumbo might have said by way of a greeting he added, 'Got the kettle on, mate?'

'No, but you can give me a ride to the Janna – I need beer!' Eric strode towards the Mercedes and Ro climbed down to shake his hand.

'This isn't a seller, is it?' Ro observed.

'No, it's Jumbo's second lorry and I'm its new driver. He's got the bit between his teeth with this Long-Haul lot and he's set another wagon on the job,' Eric informed him.

'Knowing you, I expect you worship that V8, don't you?' Ro laughed. By way of an answer, Eric faced the radiator, sank to his knees with his hands clasped together and intoned:

> 'Our manufacturer
> Which art in Sweden
> Scania be thy name
> Thy kingdom come
> Thy will be done
> In truck stops as it is in Kamyonistan.
> Give us this day our daily diesel
> And forgive us our speeding
> As we forgive them that road rage against us
> Lead us not into soft sand
> But deliver us from Haditha
> For thine is the V8
> The power and torque
> At least until Friday, amen.'

'You can't have invented that on the spot!' Ro giggled.

'True. German autobahns can be pretty boring places, you know. I had to find something to occupy the addling brain.'

'Where's Haditha?'

'Saudi side of the Jordanian border; notorious for delays.' They climbed in and Kamal was introduced.

Mehmet was pleased to see Eric, and the lunch hour became a pleasant reunion, joined by Amoun and Aysha as soon as the meal was served. 'They don't seem to be making much progress with our minaret,' Ro said during a lull in the conversation.

Compound Nouns

'That idea's been abandoned,' Mehmet said. 'Amoun heard the workmen saying that the architects had changed their minds.'

A red Land Rover pulled up outside. Two men in suits and ties got out carrying document cases. 'Speak of the devil!' Mehmet said. They shook hands with Mehmet and one of them produced a glossy magazine.

After much animated conversation, one of the men turned to Eric. 'We are honoured to meet you. I understand that you are the author of this piece here about two boys who wash trucks, using camels. What luck to find you here! We only hoped to find out where the boys had gone.'

'They're here,' Eric said, indicating Ro and Nuri.

'Oh, this is wonderful. What good fortune! Of course, I hadn't thought you'd be young men now; this magazine's two years old.' They stood up and he shook their hands warmly, introducing himself as Ismail. Amoun went off to make *shay* and the men drew up chairs. 'We are the architects who conceived this truck stop that everyone calls Kamyonistan,' Ismail continued. 'Last week, one of the members of the consortium of architects who put up the initial funding for the project, received this transport magazine here through the post. It had been sent to him by a consular official in Holland, who had been given it by the director of a haulage company who used to send their trucks to the Middle East.'

'So you're the visionaries who put this place together. I'm an enthusiastic fan of yours!' Eric gushed.

'So we see from your writing,' Ismail said. 'What we loved most about this article, though, was the way in which you pointed up the parallels we had drawn architecturally between medieval merchants and latter-day truckers with your beautiful portrayal of the young camel drivers and their truck-wash enterprise.'

'Thank you,' Eric said.

'That is precisely why we came today. We came to ensure that the presence of camels in our caravanserai-styled truck stop continues to perpetuate that sense of history for which our architecture strives.'

'But we haven't had camels for ages,' Ro said. He and Nuri explained how they made their living. Then Ismail suggested, 'If we provide you with camels, would you be prepared to look after them and perhaps find something useful for them to do?'

'I don't know when we would find the time...' Ro began.

'Of course we could,' Nuri interrupted forthrightly. 'All we would need is a regular supply of feed and a sensible place to keep the camels in.'

'Yes,' agreed Ro, uncertainly.

'Isn't this a little sentimental?' Eric suggested, tentatively.

'Yes! Of course it's sentimental!' Ismail cried, clapping Eric on the shoulders.

'This whole project has been sentimental from start to finish: it is a veritable exercise in sentimentality!'

'That's all right, then,' Eric said, and everyone laughed.

'Where to keep them, then,' Ismail said. 'What about the old livestock compound?'

'That's no good,' Nuri said. 'We need to live with them, not just go visiting them as if they were weekend ponies.'

'Well said,' Eric opined, mouthing a request for beer at Aysha, who stood in the doorway.

'What about our old corner by the minaret?' Nuri said.

'We're not restoring that minaret after all, I'm afraid,' said Ismail. 'Too expensive.'

'But you could use the stones to build a low wall and square off that corner,' Eric suggested.

'Yes, and make it include the palm tree,' Ro added.

'We can always add more palms if you want,' Ismail said. 'We have some funding in hand from the minaret project.'

'There'd have to be a shelter for the camels. We used old lorry tarpaulins, but something a bit more substantial would be better,' said Nuri.

'That's easily done. An open-fronted shelter could be built against one of the back walls,' Ismail said.

'And we'd need water plumbed across,' Nuri continued.

'That can be taken under the wall from the service road,' Ismail assured him.

'And electricity,' Ro insisted. 'We might as well live in those cabins to begin with. They've got stoves in, haven't they?'

'Yes,' Ismail said. 'As soon as we get the electricity routed to you, we'll put air-conditioning units in; it'll be unbearably hot in summer otherwise.'

'Well, well!' Mehmet laughed. 'You lot could redesign the universe in a couple of hours if you sat here long enough!'

'You'll save a fortune on rent,' Kamal said.

'If you find someone to share with you, you could take our motel room over,' Ro suggested.

'Please stay and eat with us,' Eric requested. 'It would be a pleasure to have you here a little longer. I'm dying to ask you about your original vision for a caravanserai-styled truck stop.'

The other man, who spoke no English, became engrossed in a conversation with Kamal. More food began to appear, and a wonderful sense of new opportunity and optimism pervaded the lunch party. There would be camels once again in Kamyonistan. No one was happier that day than Nuri, a cameleer through and through.

Walled Domain

Eric loaded workwear and departed on the same afternoon that Kamal moved in with Ro and Nuri. He brought a bedroll and a few clothes. Arabic lessons began that very evening. Kamal turned out to be a good teacher. He understood how language worked, and more importantly, he understood how Ro might find Arabic problematic. Nuri prepared a magnificent salad, which they shared at a leisurely pace on the roof terrace.

Each day, a new section of the wall appeared by the stunted minaret. One day a tipper arrived bearing two palm trees, which were shoehorned into holes in the ground. The camel shelter was completed by the end of the second week. During the third week, a wide gateway appeared in the line of stonework, and electricity was successfully connected. Water was supplied the following week, along with air-conditioning units and a pair of iron gates. Finally, the enclosure was planted with shrubs and some acacia bushes. The walled area was more generous than they had at first visualised, which meant that the camels would have room in which to move. Six weeks after their meeting with the architects, Ro and Nuri moved in.

'It feels strange to be sitting where we used to sit, seeing the same view across the compound, but in such a different set of circumstances,' Ro said. Nuri opened a garden chair and plonked himself beside his friend.

'It feels like another universe,' Nuri agreed. The camels had not yet arrived. Nuri was hoping to be consulted about these, but he doubted that he would be. He poured the *shay* and the sunset call to prayer rang out across the compounds. Ro's shunter stood ticking erratically, just inside the gateway. Nuri walked over to it and came back carrying a sleek case.

'You've got one of the newfangled "toplaps",' said Ro, laughing.

'Don't you mean a "taplop"?' It's my homework,' Nuri said. 'While you're up there slaving over a hot verb table with Kamal this evening, I'll make tomorrow's work easier by doing some at home. When the camels come, I'll need to do this a lot more.'

The camels did not come, however, and more weeks ticked by.

Ro relinquished his shunter for a while in order to move containers about with Rashid. Rashid was more cheerful than he had been. He showed considerable interest in the camel project, and Ro promised him that he could see them when they arrived. Rashid spoke of homesickness and recently abandoned plans to go home. It was only the thought of what they might do to him that prevented him from returning. Exile was a form of torture in its own right, he told Ro, and he felt that he had only himself to blame for it. Nonetheless, the decision not to return had taken the pressure off.

One pleasant evening, Ro went to the driver's suq for provisions. He walked, the shunter having been left in the workshop for servicing and repairs. The air was soft and as he lugged his bags home among the parked wagons, he thought of what to prepare for their evening meal. Kamal had been invited, so his lesson would be held at home for once. In the distance, he saw a small lorry pull out of the gateway to their domain. For a moment his heart raced at the memory, long ago, of such a vehicle taking Nuri away from him. He fought his sense of panic and increased his pace. Common sense told him that history would not repeat itself, that Nuri's grandfather would not be taking him away again; and that in any case Nuri was now old enough and assertive enough to foil such an attempt. Ro told himself to try not to be so emotionally dependent on Nuri. What if he died? How would Ro be prepared for such an event? He knew that he would go to pieces. His sense of panic rose again and he almost ran the last few metres. The gates were shut. Ro let himself in and went to the kitchen to deposit the food.

'Nuri!' he called. 'I'm back.' He put the perishables in the refrigerator and called again. Then he climbed the outside stairs to the bedroom and sitting room. It was deserted. He descended into the area they had started to call the garden and made his way to the shelter. The first sight that met his eyes was a tall, beautifully coated camel. Next to her was a tiny baby camel. Engrossed in bonding with the little camel was Nuri.

A few days later, they received a visit from Ismail. He seemed pleased with the progress of their plans. In the back of the Land Rover were the saddle, saddlebags and paraphernalia belonging to the mother camel. 'Short of recommencing your camel-assisted truck wash, I'm not sure what you're going to do with these,' Ismail said. 'I'm sure you'll think of something.'

'Kamal does his rounds on a motorcycle,' Nuri said. 'I thought of doing mine by camel, but it'll be some time yet before the baby can be left. At first, I would have to take him along too, attached to his mother.'

'Yes indeed, he needs to do some growing first,' agreed Ismail. 'Ask your friend Eric to take some pictures, will you? I'll try and get something in the architectural press.'

'I hope Ismail isn't going to turn us into some tasteless theme-park attraction,' Ro said. 'I'd want to run a mile.'

'Me too,' said Nuri.

'What are these in Arabic, again?' Ro asked, picking up the canvas panniers.

'*Kurj*,' Nuri answered.

'Ah, yes, I remember now. You've not talked about your idea about being a camel-mounted courier before, Nuri. When did you think of that?'

'Just now,' Nuri said. 'With these *kurj*, I could do several sets of papers at a time.'

'Will KLHS wear it?'

'They'll accept it from a man like Ismail,' Nuri said simply.

'We'll have to protect Dabus from getting run over,' Ro said. 'He's only little. Come on, let's light a fire outside like we used to when we had the lorry.'

'We haven't got *hattab* – firewood.'

'We used to collect it using the camels,' Ro said.

'Let's do that now. They need a walk,' Nuri said, excitedly.

The she-camel bellowed and roared with protest at being saddled up, but once she was on her feet Nuri attached the infant to her by a rope and she settled down. It surprised them how much scrap wood was lying around. Some of it was under trailers or against the wall. Much of it was simply pressed into the ground by lorries. 'There never used to be this much,' Nuri said.

'The place was full of refugees, remember? It was always a bit of a scramble for firewood, especially in the winter.'

'Do you think those stoves will be warm enough when the cold comes?' Nuri said.

'Blimey, I hope so!' Ro stuffed another shard of pallet wood into the saddlebag. The graceful camel bristled with firewood.

'We haven't much kindling,' Nuri said.

'We'll split some of this up.'

After dark, they sat preparing their meal by the fire. The camels crouched nearby. Nuri sang softly in Arabic and watched the flying sparks extinguish themselves high above the embers. They heard the gate swing. A moment later, Amoun, Aysha carrying Azhar, Rashid, Mahmout and Kamal stepped into the firelight, bearing contributions of various foods. The evening meal was transformed into a barbecue and they all chattered happily into the night.

Also chattering happily into the night, many miles away, were Bingo and his passenger, Titania 'I'm-getting-too-old-for-this-lark' Roberts. They had parked the wagon in the customs TIR park in Sibiu, Romania, and were sitting in a pleasant restaurant terrace in the town centre. The streets thronged with people strolling, dining or drinking. It had been an arduous drive from the border. Despite huge improvements, Romania's roads still required much concentration at the wheel. 'Unlit horses and carts on the main roads used to be one of the worst hazards,' Bingo explained. 'They seem to be confined to the side roads and towns now.'

'We could be in the Campo di Fiori in Rome!' Titania laughed as a quartet of gypsy-looking musicians struck up with a collection of beautiful Romanian café songs.

'Or Kamyonistan!' Bingo said. 'Here, have a drop more red diesel.' He topped up Titania's glass with some very respectable Romanian wine.

'I half expect to see dancing bears,' Titania said.

'There used to be one on the Bulgarian side of the Danube at

Ruse,' Bingo said. 'But I haven't seen it for a long time. There was one at the Harem truck stop in Istanbul, too.'

'I suppose EU status will put a stop to all that.'

'Tomorrow we brave the Bucharest ring road,' said Bingo. 'I hope it's in better repair than it used to be. Mind you, there are one or two good Turk-parks on it.'

Their food arrived and for a while they soaked in the atmosphere. 'Penny for your thoughts, driver?' Titania said.

'I was just thinking about the boys and their new camels,' answered Bingo.

'I do hope it works out for them down there,' Titania said. 'They seem to be settling. It just seems a pity that they have to live in such an unsettled part of the world.'

'And does any town in England on a Friday night seem to you like a settled part of the world?' Bingo asked.

'No,' replied Titania. 'Shall we have another bottle and live up to our reputation?'

'How good are you at weeing into empty water bottles in a dark lorry cab when inebriated?' Bingo asked.

'Let's just order another glass, then!' Titania laughed. 'Anyway, it'll be lovely to see the boys again.'

'You'll find them very self-assured young men now,' said Bingo. He ordered a second bottle anyway, but resisted the temptation to ask for a funnel.

Far, far away, Aysha was running Azhar's little hand through the soft hair of the baby camel. In a truck stop on the outskirts of Thessaloniki, Jumbo was swilling retsina and tucking into an almost palatable steak, his lorry pointing south. Eric was driving out of Calais into a black night in which rain blew horizontally across the road in front of the windscreen. It would be a long night, but he hoped to make Macon by lunchtime. One way or another, everyone was heading for Kamyonistan.

The Wedding Party

The wedding guests spilled out of the drivers' mosque into the late afternoon sunshine. It was an unusual mixture of people. They had turned out to witness, sanction or bless the marriage of Amoun to Aysha, both Palestinian refugees and unofficial immigrants in Kamyonistan. Their consistently responsible attitude to Azhar, to each other, to Mehmet and to the Kamyonistan community had earned them sufficient respect to make the case for marriage. It was a truncated affair, dispensing with niceties like dowries, parents to give them away and the usual family infrastructure so essentially part of a Middle-East wedding. Mehmet wore a suit, along with Jumbo, whose suit had lain dormant under his lorry bunk since Nuri's asylum hearing. Bingo and Titania looked presentable after a visit to the suq, and Rashid managed to look dashing in a long-sleeved white shirt. Mahmout and Kamal wore sports jackets and jeans, while Ro and Nuri went identically clad in white jalabiyas with red and white *shamaghs*. Eric came as he was. The happy couple wore matching denim suits, to which Aysha had added a white headscarf, while baby Azhar wore the brown and white *shamagh* into which he had been born. Last-minute witnesses and stragglers included a Jordanian driver and his assistant, two Turkish drivers who were regulars in the Janna, and the receptionist from the little clinic where Azhar was taken for check-ups. Henna had been found for the ladies' hands.

They emerged smiling from wedding prayers that had been conducted by the sympathetic imam with whom Ro and Nuri already had a good relationship. Shoes were put back on and a noisy procession made its way to the Janna for the wedding feast. As they set foot on the veranda, the Kamyonistan café band launched into a medley of appropriate tunes. The party had started.

The Wedding Party

'Do you think the band will play for our wedding, Nuri?' Ro whispered. Nuri looked at him uncomprehendingly. A burly man in a greasy dark jacket shouldered his way through the throng. It was the gate man. He handed Amoun a gift-wrapped parcel and hugged him.

'I've dragged you out of trailers more times than there are ants!' he said, and turned to go.

'Wait!' Amoun cried. 'Fetch your wife and join us!'

Jumbo handed Eric a beer over the heads of the Turkish drivers upon whom Kamal was sharpening his Turkish. 'There you go, mate,' Jumbo said, handing the Turks their beers. He turned to Kamal and said, 'More Turks have dug me out of the shit than any other nationality on the road.'

Rashid ambled over, clutching a beer. He pulled up a chair next to Jumbo, who said, 'Hello, long time no see! I must congratulate you on your work with young Ro over there. You've trained him well: I reckon he could back an artic into the crack of a man's arse if he bent over long enough!'

'Now, now, Jumbo; are you being vulgar again?' Titania giggled, squeezing in next to him.

'I was just complimenting the ayatollah here on his driving instruction,' Jumbo boomed.

Ro talked to Mahmout by the counter. 'I've been doing up the little office at the truck wash,' Mahmout told him. 'There's a sofa there and everything. Do you want to come and see it?' Ro wondered why he kept thinking of swarthy knees. He hesitated before saying vaguely, 'No. Later maybe.'

Bingo took his place and Ro went in search of Nuri. Nuri held Azhar and answered Aysha's questions about the rearing of baby camels. Amoun was helping Mehmet to keep the show on the road. The band played on while Eric plied them with drinks before talking to Titania. 'I think people just see us gliding serenely by in our hi-tech cabs and do not realise that our bodies are in a ceaseless dynamic state: each tiny muscle constantly adjusting to, compensating for and accommodating the motions of roll, pitch, bounce, yaw, shudder, swing and wallow,' Eric said, earnestly. 'Poor road surfaces, buffeting winds and hard braking, steering or accelerating can exaggerate and combine these characteristics alarmingly, even in a new wagon, with quite fatiguing results.'

'You really know how to chat a girl up, don't you!' Titania laughed. 'What do think about in bed?'

'Oh... my mind goes blank!' Eric replied.

The KLHS traffic manager, Fahmy, turned up for his 'quick one' before going home. He often worked through the weekend, so no one was surprised to see him. Jumbo stood him a drink and talked shop for a while. Then Fahmy collared Kamal, Ro and Nuri, ushering them onto the veranda. 'Here, these are for you,' he said, producing a clutch of mobile phones and presenting them to the boys. 'This is so that I can keep in touch with you around the place. We've had a bit of trouble coordinating the more itinerant members of staff since the big move, and as the police don't like us using short-wave radios, we're issuing these. No long international calls, though, please – or you'll be buying your own cards.'

'What do you think of the idea of Nuri using a camel instead of a moped to do his rounds with?' Ro asked. 'It's got saddlebags for paperwork.'

'Ismail, the architect, is keen on the idea,' Nuri put in, quickly.

'I can't see why not.' Fahmy laughed. 'We can always try it and see. If it flops, we'll abandon it. I quite like the thought. Do you want it painted up in KLHS livery?'

'Imagine doing that in the UK!' Eric roared, when Ro told him the news. 'The Health and Safety Executive would have a nervous breakdown!'

'If the animal rights terrorists didn't kill everyone first!' said Jumbo.

'If we didn't get outlawed for daring to say as much, by the politically correct brigade even before that!' Bingo added.

'Don't get excited, boys!' Titania said. 'It's all swings and roundabouts, remember. You can't take camels into the transport hub at home, but you can write to your local paper and sound off about it, ripping into every authority in sight. You can't do that here.'

'All right, miss, but can we have our marbles back at playtime?' Bingo said and everyone laughed.

The Wedding Party

The double-bass player ambled over and Bingo went to get him a drink. 'Do you normally play in Damascus?' Titania asked him. His English was very hesitant, but he managed to convey that they did a number of gigs each week in various cafés, bars, academic campuses and restaurants. She told him how she marvelled at the variety of styles they could manage. The player turned to Bingo, who had arrived with the drinks. Out of the corner of her eye, Titania caught sight of Aysha, who was leaning rearwards with her hands on the small of her back. She wondered if Aysha was pregnant. Another infant of Azhar's calibre would be a gift indeed, but a lot of hard work for the struggling newlyweds. She decided to keep 'mum' about her hunch. Amoun approached Aysha with the baby. Azhar kissed the bride, and several people clapped. Azhar giggled and sneezed into her neck. Titania decided it was time for gin and tonic. She'd have to go to the lorry for that, and she slid the keys from Bingo's pocket.

On the veranda, she found Ro consoling Rashid, who was suffering from a depressive relapse. 'Tell him to stop drinking!' she whispered to Ro. 'Alcoholic depression only makes real depression worse. I'm just off to find the gin – see you later.'

'Mahmout invited me to see his new office sofa,' Ro told Nuri.

'Do you think it was a come-on?' Nuri asked.

'It might have been.'

'Why are you telling me?'

'I was just thinking; what if we both went? It wouldn't be infidelity then, would it?'

'I don't know. What about AIDS?'

'We don't have to do anything too intimate.'

'What about Bingo?'

'He only has casual sex with him. There's no relationship there.'

'How do you know?'

'I don't. We could ask him. Here he is now. Bingo, do you just have a casual relationship with Mahmout, or are you in a proper relationship?'

'What sort of question is that, you nosey little sod?' Bingo laughed. 'I'm not about to take him back and set up home with him, if that's what you mean.'

The Wedding Party

'Casual, then,' Ro said.

'Yes. If you like,' replied Bingo. 'Now where did I put my beer?'

'When Palestine is finally set up,' Kamal was telling Aysha, 'it will be important for people like you and Amoun to go back and help rebuild it.'

'But look what happened in Iraq,' Aysha protested. 'The people who had stuck it out at home spurned the exiles and expats. They tried to prevent them from doing anything to help rebuild the country.'

'That was only the political leaders,' Kamal said. 'Ordinary people won't be viewed with such suspicion.'

'There'll be an awful lot of us returning. We'll swamp the place. That's bound to cause unrest,' Aysha said. 'Anyway, with the Israelis building more settlements instead of negotiating for peace, Hamas launching rockets instead of laying down arms, and Americans bungling negotiations, I'll be a grandmother before anything useful happens.'

Ro nearly collided with Titania, who was carrying a soft drinks can. 'I thought you didn't drink that "chemical rubbish", Titania,' he said. Ro took the can from her and sniffed it. '*Gin!*' he exclaimed. 'In a lemonade can?'

'Old drivers' trick,' Titania confided, giving a theatrical wink.

'Which old driver did you have in mind?'

'Kees actually! You remember the Dutch driver who was killed with your uncle Norman. Him, he used to do it,' Titania said.

A ringtone sounded shrilly from Ro's pocket. He drew it out and clamped it to his ear. A booming voice said, 'Quick! Get that shunter wound up, laddie, there are twenty trailers to be moved. We've been looking for you everywhere!' Ro looked across the veranda and saw Jumbo's form in the doorway, holding Nuri's phone to his ear. They laughed.

'Nuri's language is all over the place,' Kamal confided to Bingo, good-naturedly. 'When he retrieves paperwork from the Turkish drivers, he uses Turkish, two kinds of Arabic, and English! I'm going to compile *The Kamyonistani Phrase Book*, by Kamal of Damascus. I could make a fortune!'

The band turned up the volume. Mehmet chatted to the gate man's wife, while the gate man chatted to Amoun. The night was yet young.

School Delivery

Bingo had taken his unit to the workshops for minor repairs. Ro was backing Bingo's empty trailer onto the loading bay. His mobile phone warbled and he answered it. 'Ro!' Fahmy's voice said. 'We've got an irate Englishman in the office and we think you might be able to help us, as you speak the language.'

'I'll be two minutes,' Ro said. He dropped the trailer and pulled the unit out before heading back to the traffic office, trying to imagine whom this English driver might be. Tied to the camel bar of a dead shunter outside the office was Nuri's new courier transport, attached to which was its offspring. He parked a little distance downwind of the camels to spare them the exhaust fumes and went inside.

Fahmy looked harassed. 'Ah good,' he said. 'This is Ron…'

'That's right,' Ron cut in, with a crisp northern accent. 'My house contents were removed from England and deposited here several months ago. A company called Kamyonistan-TIR stored them and were supposed to deliver them. I understand that Kamyonistan-TIR were taken over by this outfit here.'

'That's right,' Ro said.

'Well, laddie, they've just delivered the stuff to my house in Damascus but it's not all there. There's an important piece missing.'

'Any idea what it is?'

'Of course I've any idea what it is! That's why I'm here,' Ron said rudely. 'Now you'd better get your arse in gear and find the bloody thing before I start reading the Riot Act!'

'What are we looking for, then?' Ro asked, calmly.

'A piano! How you can lose a flaming piano, I don't know, but you've managed it somehow,' Ron fumed.

'A *piano*?' The truth began to dawn on Ro. In view of the man's rude manner, he put aside his tact and diplomacy and said

School Delivery

sweetly, 'I know where we can find your piano, sir. How was life in prison?'

'What?' Ron shouted. Then he stopped himself and adopted a more conciliatory tone. 'Right then, perhaps you'll be so kind as to show it to me and we'll get this thing sorted out once and for all.'

'I can do better than that,' Ro said, wishing to prevent Ron from seeing his precious beer-stained piano lounging in the Janna. 'I can have it delivered to you immediately. We put that piano aside for safe keeping. You can't just leave a piano lying around with dangerous goods and things, you know.'

'Right. It hasn't to go to my home address. I can't play the piano. It's to go to a new international school in Damascus. I work there, so I brought the piano as household goods rather than have the school import it. Here's the address, on this business card.' He handed Ro the card.

'Thank you, Ro. Well done!' Fahmy said, when Ron had departed. 'I'll send you with the driver who delivers the piano, just to make sure all goes well.' Ro went outside into the hot sunshine. It was nearly time to pick up Nuri for lunch. He couldn't wait to tell Bingo about the piano. News of its owner's irascible demeanour might assuage Bingo's guilt about having misappropriated it in the first place, he thought, chuckling to himself.

A local driver, Mustafa, was assigned the task of delivering the piano. It was secured to the tail end of a tilt, which seemed to swallow up this single item. The driver was apprehensive about taking Titania, who had insisted on accompanying the piano. It tickled her to think of herself as a piano accompaniment, and in any case she was interested to meet the irascible teacher and see inside the new international school. 'Sheer nosiness!' was how Bingo described her foray. She sat in the passenger seat of the Russian-built Maz unit, while Ro crouched on the bunk.

The traffic thickened as they entered the outskirts of the city. Two little boys driving a cart piled high with rubbish and pulled by two long-eared donkeys came against the flow, in the opposite direction. They were deep in conversation and were gesticulating theatrically at one another.

'How do I know if there are footballs in paradise?' the older one was saying.

'Marbles, then?'

'Marbles? What would an angel want with marbles?'

'To play with, of course!'

'I don't think angels play. They're more like grown-ups, really.'

'What about child ones? Don't they want to play?'

'I don't suppose for one minute you'd get child angels.'

'Don't children die, then? That boy in the shanty town died last week just coughing!'

'All right, then: there might be children who are angels, but I don't think dead people just turn into angels automatically.'

'Why not?'

'They have to be converted first. You know, adjusted.'

'Like when one-eyed Uncle Mohammed puts cooking oil in the taxi instead of diesel?'

'Yes. Exactly like that.'

The school was in a quiet, respectable residential area. It still had a bit of a building site feel about it, as if it were nearing completion. Having got past a very thorough gate man, they were greeted by the principal himself. Titania found him charming and attentive. While Mustafa and Ro struggled with the instrument, Titania was whisked away for a tour of the premises. The piano was installed in a beautifully appointed music room, where a class of six-year-olds were learning a song about slurping spaghetti. 'Does your mum give you spaghetti?' the teacher asked them.

'No,' said one.

'What does your mum make for you, then?'

'Chicken stew. My mum gives me nice food to grow me.'

'What, like a little tomato plant?' The teacher smiled kindly. The child nodded. Ro felt slightly overwhelmed by being plunged into a school atmosphere that seemed quite at variance with life at Kamyonistan Long-Haul Services. He hadn't set foot in a school since that Christmas he had gone to hunt for Nuri in Sinai.

Titania hadn't set foot in one recently either: not since her retirement from Indigo Lane School for Girls. This was a lovely school, she thought. The corridors thronged with ex-pat children of various nationalities. There seemed to be plenty of Syrian children too. 'I wish you every success with this venture,' she told the principal when they returned to the lorry. 'You have a very nice school here.'

'Well, remember: if you fancy a spell out of retirement, I'm sure we could find you a post here, with your experience. Don't forget to email your CV to me.'

'OK,' Titania said. 'But I can't promise you anything. I'm rather enjoying retirement, you know!'

'Between you and me, it's still unofficial, but there may be a short contract for maternity cover arising in the junior music department after half-term if you're interested,' said the principal, beaming.

Mustafa started the engine and drew the truck forwards to enable Ro to close up the back of the trailer. Ro tucked the TIR cord into the staples and wiped his hands on his trousers. 'Come on then, teach!' he said saucily to Titania, giving the principal a farewell wave.

Arm in arm, they strolled down the side of the lorry to the cab. 'Strange for both of us, eh? Being back at school...' Titania said, and Ro nodded.

Arriving back in the parking compound, Ro caught sight of Nuri in the distance, leading the camels through the dust. It caught him unawares and for a fraction of a second, a million memories spilled through his mind and he gasped. Then his heart melted at the grace of both boy and camels. Titania was saying something. 'Are you listening to me, Ro?' she said.

'Sorry. I was miles away...'

'I was just saying that the principal was surprised that the authorities were so relaxed about Bingo and me sharing a lorry cab, even though we aren't married.'

'So am I, but I didn't like to say,' Ro said.

'What is Bingo's surname?' Titania asked.

'Guagewick?' Ro ventured.

'No, silly, that's Jumbo's name.'

'I don't think I've ever known it. It's not part of his email address.'

'It is Roberts,' Titania said.

School Delivery

'Same as yours, then!' Ro laughed.

'Exactly. They think we're married.'

'Nice one! Shall I drop you off at Bingo's unit? He's got the kettle on, look.'

Bingo Roberts chinked mugs with Titania Roberts. He was stripped to the waist and smudgy from scrambling about between the chassis rails. 'Well, I think you ought to drop everything and go. A term won't kill you. It'll be a good experience, and you can keep in touch with these youngsters here,' Bingo said.

'What about my house? I couldn't face packing everything into storage, and I really don't fancy letting it out,' Titania protested.

'Let me house-sit for you,' Bingo said. 'I'm ready for a move, as you know. It's got far too noisy of late. People are changing. Only ten to fifteen years ago, it used to be silent after eleven at night. Now, people sound their car horns day and night, have loud music day and night and scream at each other day and night.'

'Have you got a lot of foreigners, then?'

'No! They're all English!' Bingo said. 'Selfish through and through.'

'I suppose this is the generation of children who sat in front of the telly instead of going out to play, learning how to be good neighbours,' Titania said.

'So are you going to teach in Damascus or aren't you?' Bingo asked.

'I'll sleep on it. I can't send in my CV till I get home, anyway,' said Titania, holding her mug out. 'Can I have secs, please?'

'Sex?' Bingo said, aghast.

'It's short for "seconds"!' Titania laughed. 'The girls used to say it at school, lining up for their dinners. The dinner ladies always pretended to be suitably shocked.'

She watched Ro's shunter make its way across the compound towards Nuri and the camels. Cocking her head on one side, she observed Ro climb out of the cab, walk over to Nuri, give him a heartfelt hug, climb back into his unit and drive back the way he had come. 'I wonder what that was all about?' she said.

'I wonder,' Bingo smiled. He'd seen it too.

'Bless their little hearts,' Titania said softly. 'We've a lot of food that wants using up; shall we have a cook-up by the lorries tonight?'

School Delivery

'Righto!'

Nuri snuggled up to Ro in the dark. It had gone midnight. A cock had crowed prematurely. 'Ro?' he whispered.

'What?'

'Do you still want to share Mahmout with me?'

'No, Nuri; when I saw you with the camels in the parking today, I knew that it was only you that I wanted.'

'Good.'

'Night, night.'

'Ro?'

'Yes, I do love you. Night, night.'

Responses

Rashid's shunter had given up the ghost and Fahmy had put him in Ro's. This meant that Ro had to assist him again, and to Ro's dismay, Rashid required a fair bit of assistance. By lunchtime each day, Rashid was drunk. No one was quite sure who was supplying him. He had taken a leaf out of Titania's book and appeared to have an endless supply of canned soft drinks heavily laced with vodka. His gentle persona was lost in the mists of his evaporating self. He strode into the Janna with Ro, barking overconfidently about the company. Mehmet served them food on the veranda. For half an hour he hooted and boasted about all the things he could do, should anyone ever threaten his sense of security. The following half-hour was spent exploring wild conspiracy theories during which his bravado spiralled rapidly downwards into a mire of fearful and paranoid speculations about who might be watching him. This wasn't the case of a boozy driver spending thirty years imperceptibly sliding down the slippery slope into functional alcoholism; rather it was the case of a driver hitherto unaccustomed to drink charging headlong into serious bingeing.

Mehmet suggested to Ro that it would sort itself out because his Iranian colleagues would put him right. Rashid, however, was too smart for that. Knowing that he had already gradually isolated himself from them he also remained careful not to appear drunk in front of them. This further isolated him. His driving became erratic and he began to make careless mistakes with the trailers. But for Ro's efficiency in matching up the paperwork, trailers and loads, Rashid's condition might have come to light sooner than it did. Ro was becoming worn down by the endless boring rhetoric, psychotic tale-telling, and the stench of alcohol-laced cigarette smoke in the hot cab.

One unpleasantly muggy lunch hour, Rashid parked the shunter with a very heavily laden trailer outside the restaurant. 'I reckon there's at least thirty-five tonnes on that trailer,' Rashid barked. His eyes were unfocussed and the quality of his voice was distorted. Ro felt that he was with a parody of Rashid and he began to wonder where the real one had gone.

'Chicken *tawwuk* for me and the boy here!' Rashid boomed at Mehmet, tapping sharply on the counter with his keys. Ro remembered a time when he would have been referred to respectfully, not as 'the boy here'; and he would have been consulted as to what he wanted to eat.

Aysha came out and popped Azhar's cot on the veranda. 'It's getting too hot in that kitchen for him. Isn't it muggy today!' she said to Ro. Rashid fixed his eyes on her rear end as she left and uttered something lascivious in Farsi.

Aysha returned with the condiments and some water. Then she looked up and screamed. It was no scream of distress, but a blood-curdling scream that foreshadowed unthinkable chaos. Ro screwed round just in time to see the heavy lorry smash, trailer first, into the veranda. The sickening sound of splintering wood and Aysha's screams blotted out the other senses. He felt the whole building shake. Then he heard Aysha shrieking Azhar's name.

Ro leapt to the rear of the trailer where it had come to rest, having crushed pillars, tables and chairs in its path. Mehmet and Amoun were by his side within seconds. Rashid stumbled and fell over chairs as he tottered to the scene of devastation. There was no sign of Azhar or his cot. Mehmet began to invoke the name of Allah in every possible configuration he could think of. The death of a parent is expected, but no one gets over the death of a child, he reflected; and at that moment of empathy with Aysha he was overcome with panic.

'You must have left the handbrake off, Ro,' a voice slurred behind Ro.

Ro spun round alarmed, but Amoun was there, glaring into Rashid's face. 'I watched you get out of the driver's seat, you drunken bastard, and if that baby's dead, so are you!' he snarled savagely.

Ro crawled under the back of the trailer. The overhang to the rear of the wheels had ridden over the floorboards of the veranda.

'Was the baby on a table?' Ro called to Aysha. He heard her scream afresh. Then silence. Amoun's voice said, 'She says she put him on the floor.'

'There's no spare wheel carrier on this trailer. There's a chance he might be trapped underneath!' Ro shouted. Amoun went to his side and crawled underneath with Ro.

'If only we could get the trailer up a bit... I'll see if I can raise it on the air system,' Ro said. He searched the chassis for the controls. Then he noticed the beefy-looking leaf springs. 'No good, Amoun; it's an older trailer. No airbags.' He ran back to Amoun.

'Can we get under the floorboards, Mehmet?' Amoun said. 'There's a chance they might be broken here. We might be able to get at the space from underneath.'

'Wait,' Ro said. He called Rashid. Rashid had disappeared. Ro faced Amoun, his eyes shining. 'Amoun. Remember that time, a long time ago, when you hid in a garment trailer and the refugees set fire to it?'

'Yes.'

'Well, Tariq and Ahmad had disconnected the trailer so that when the Turk pulled away, the trailer fell on its knees and the rear of the trailer ended up in the air,' Ro said. Mehmet returned with a variety of old tools and, with Aysha helping him, he began to hack at the floor behind the trailer.

Ro and Amoun ran to the tractor unit. Ro fired up the engine while Amoun disconnected the air lines. Then Ro pulled the turntable pin and revved the engine. When the air pressure was up, he released the handbrake. The trailer was heavy, however, and instead of allowing the unit to slide out, it pressed down on it and held it in place. Ro gave it some power and the wheels began to spin on the soft ground. He tried to snatch at it by letting the clutch out quickly. It stalled. He tried again. It stalled. Then it nearly failed to start again because the battery was no good. Ro started the engine once more. A red light came on and a buzzer sounded: the air had gone. He built the air up again. Once more he tried to snatch at it, but let the clutch out a little more gently than before, hitting the throttle at the same time. The unit shot out from under the trailer and the trailer lurched forward onto its front, lower edge. Ro leapt out of the cab and ran with Amoun to the rear of the trailer, which now hung perilously in the air, taking part of the veranda roof with it.

They scrambled and dug frantically with their hands in the debris. Just as Amoun had predicted, the floor had caved in where the trailer had come to rest. In the semi-darkness of the cavity, nestling between two joists, was the cot. Amoun pulled it out. It was empty. Ro could not bear the look of panic in his eyes. Amoun had saved this baby from death under a trailer on the day it was born. This seemed too cruel a fate for the little soul. Then Ro saw that where the cot had been there was a *shamagh*. He reached in, dreading what might meet his fingers. Ro lifted out the bundle and handed it to Amoun. Tears were already streaming down Amoun's face as he unwound the filthy *shamagh*. Inside, was Azhar – asleep. It was the most precious sight Amoun had ever witnessed or would probably ever witness again. He lifted his head to call for Aysha, but the words would not come and he just sobbed instead. Ro scrambled out to find Aysha.

Rashid was never seen again. Ro was promoted from assistant shunter to shunter proper, and a party was held at the Janna to celebrate Azhar's deliverance.

Paradise Debunked

Eric, Bingo and Jumbo, having loaded in the same Kamyonistan factory for the same freight forwarder, KLHS, found themselves on the same 'shift' as one another. KLHS loaded them in Manchester and sent them back out to Syria and they ran together all the way down. On his top bunk, Bingo carried two suitcases of teaching materials and domestic essentials belonging to Titania, who had accepted the temporary maternity cover in Damascus.

On their first evening back in Kamyonistan, it rained. Late sunshine tried in vain to break through. Nonetheless, they dined on the veranda. 'I declare the meeting open,' Jumbo announced, raising his beer.

'What meeting?' Ro asked.

'The paradise club of course! We're nearly all here. Blimey, look at that rain; it's coming down in stair rods!'

'Showing your age there,' Bingo said.

'Why?'

'When did you last see a stair rod?'

'Huh. It'll be a sea of mud out there tomorrow,' Jumbo grumbled.

'Ro! Tell us again about baby Azhar and the trailer. It all came out a bit jumbled last time. I want the full story. Shame there's no picture of the capsized trailer: it would have made a good article,' Eric said. Ro then retold the news of Azhar's rescue.

'We'll make a trucker out of you yet!' Eric said at the end. 'It's a terrible thing, though, alcohol addiction.'

'All addiction is,' said Bingo. 'The trouble is, I'm coming to the conclusion that all addicts are in pursuit of paradise.'

'What?' Jumbo said.

'Think about it: alcoholics, chocoholics, workaholics, shopaholics and sexoholics are all after one thing – paradise,' Bingo said.

'Along with all the other druggies,' Eric added.

'But we're not addicts just because we're interested in paradise, are we?' Ro protested.

'I'm not so sure,' Bingo answered, uneasily. 'We may be paradise addicts along with the rest of them.'

'Heresy!' Eric exclaimed. 'Burn him at the stake!'

'Let his pigeons out!' Jumbo laughed. Then he added, 'I suppose you could claim that religious fanatics were paradise addicts.'

'And you could add that all religious people are,' Bingo said.

'Karl Marx's notion that religion is the opium of the masses?' Eric asked. Bingo nodded. In the distance, Nuri could be seen plodding home late from work with the she-camel. He had been weaning the baby off its mother, which had made him a little more efficient out there in the compounds.

'At least you can't get addicted to Kamyonistan,' Ro said cheerfully. There was a long silence.

'But we probably are addicted to Kamyonistan,' Bingo said gloomily.

'That's ridiculous,' Jumbo said.

'It's not,' said Bingo. 'In one way or another, you, me, Eric, Nuri, Ro, Amoun, Mehmet and Titania are addicted to Kamyonistan. Look at the extent to which we have physically, mentally and emotionally invested in it. We keep coming back for more, no matter what.'

'Oh, I think that's taking it a bit far,' said Eric.

'I reckon we're all addicted to Kamyonistan and we each have our own angle on it – our own subsidiary addiction,' persisted Bingo.

'What's mine, then?' Eric challenged.

'Wagons,' Bingo said. 'You're addicted to Kamyonistan in general and lorries in particular. Eric said nothing and Bingo continued. 'I am addicted to Kamyonistan in general and the Middle-East run in particular; Ro is addicted to Kamyonistan in general and Nuri in particular…'

'That's different,' Ro protested.

'It isn't. Be honest! Nuri isn't addicted to you. He loves you best in the world, but he's not addicted to you like you are to him.

Emotionally, you are utterly dependent on him,' Bingo said candidly. Ro scowled. Bingo rolled on like a juggernaut. 'Jumbo here,' he continued, 'is addicted to Kamyonistan in general and beer in particular; or to be fair in his case, the whole social ambience that goes with swilling beer in the Janna. Titania is addicted to Kamyonistan in general and the community in particular. Mehmet is addicted to Kamyonistan in general and the restaurant in particular. Amoun is addicted to Kamyonistan in general and baby Azhar in particular.'

'You can't call that addiction,' Eric protested. 'Kamyonistan's just a place.'

'It's not just a place,' Bingo said. 'It's a magical oasis we've constructed in our minds. It's our holiday condominium on the Costa del Fortune; it's the desert island in the South Seas…'

'What's wrong with that?' Jumbo asked.

'Nothing is necessarily wrong with it, as long as you see nothing necessarily wrong with addiction,' Bingo said.

'So we're addicted to a dream, right?' Eric challenged.

'I'm just suggesting that we may all be addicted to an illusion,' Bingo answered.

'The illusion of paradise?' Eric said. 'But we have never questioned that paradise might be an illusion. What you now seem to be suggesting is that paradise is a delusion, because it is tainted with the shame of addiction.'

'I am, indeed, suggesting that all those who follow the great religions, who take mood-altering substances, from sugar to heroin, who indulge in the delights of Greater Kamyonistan or who desire congress with all and sundry, are collectively in pursuit of the illusion – or possibly delusion – of paradise,' Bingo said.

'What's wrong with that, if it makes us happy?' Jumbo asked.

'Yes,' Eric agreed.

'But is it real happiness?' Bingo asked.

'That may not matter,' Eric said. 'If addiction is such a powerful part of the human condition, might it be part of our survival kit? A man obsessively stockpiling firewood in the gloom of a November afternoon is surely no more of a wood addict than a squirrel hoarding nuts on the same afternoon is a nut addict.'

Nuri, drenched, raised his hand in silent greeting and plonked himself in a cane chair. 'Nuri, are you addicted to Kamyonistan in general and addicted to camels in particular?' Ro asked, with a hint of rebellion in his voice.

'Yes,' answered Nuri.

'Why?'

'Because Kamyonistan gives me shelter and security and the camels earn me my bread.' Nuri answered.

'I rest my case,' Eric said. Amoun appeared at the table in order to collect crockery. A cigarette protruded from his mouth. Eric watched him and said, 'Are you addicted to cigarettes, Amoun?'

'Yes,' he said. 'They help me to survive the day.'

'Like taking candy from a baby,' Eric smiled. He turned to Bingo. 'OK, Bingo: what if we took away these addictive props? What would be left?'

'In Rashid's case, he'd either be forced to seek other ways of coping with his pain or he'd commit suicide,' Bingo said bluntly. 'Your life without lorries or Kamyonistan; Ro's without Nuri or Kamyonistan; Jumbo's without the Janna or Kamyonistan; Amoun's without Azhar or Kamyonistan; mine without the Middle-East run or Kamyonistan and so on and so forth, would leave each of us dependent upon our inner resources to survive differently. In other words, not being addicted might be just as essential to our survival as being addicted. Therefore, addiction may only be an incidental tool in the survival kit, and not as vital as you suggest.'

'When's Titania arriving?' asked Ro, changing the subject. Jumbo shuffled and looked relieved.

Bingo snapped out of his thinking capsule and said, 'She'll be here tomorrow. The plane lands at midday. She'll be met by the school and taken to her apartment. Tomorrow evening I'll run these cases down to the school in the unit. If the flat is easy enough to find, I might even get a taxi and take the cases straight to her.'

'Better not break the news to her that the paradise club has debunked paradise until she's settled in,' Eric said, sardonically.

'Cheer up, Eric.' Bingo grinned. 'We've only challenged it – we haven't shattered any holy grails, yet.'

'I might give up camels and take up beer instead,' said Nuri, suddenly. Everyone laughed.

Culture Shock

'You've chosen a right old time to come, haven't you?' a raven-haired woman in her forties called to Titania across the staffroom.

'What do you mean? I'm Titania, by the way,' Titania answered with a wave. The woman waved a newspaper back at her and said, 'I'm Doreen. Haven't you seen today's headlines about Syria bracing itself for an invasion?'

'That'll be the Americans again,' said Titania, laughing. 'It'll be bluff. After Iraq, they'd never be so stupid as to do it again!'

'I wouldn't be so sure,' Doreen said. 'You've got mine after play. They're Year Three. There are only fifteen of them. Good as gold.'

Titania received them in the music room and introduced herself to the eager little faces gazing up at her from the carpet. When she had retired, she had been teaching teenagers, and it was some years since she had taught the primary age group. Nonetheless, she certainly had not lost her magic and the art of cherishing and nurturing young children, and guiding them through their school day returned to her as quickly as riding a bicycle might have done. Unlike riding a bike, however, she had forgotten how exhausting it was to be constantly meeting the needs of children. Titania had arrived armed to the teeth with good, fun songs to sing. Many of them were 'rounds', and some of them were simple part songs.

The children loved them, and by the end of the first week, parents were making special detours to her classroom to thank her for the happy gift of music that she was sharing with their offspring. She revived recorder playing, developed percussion sessions and rehearsed the school orchestra. Assemblies were utilised for performances. On the playground among the palms and lemon trees, she taught them to sing sweetly, to live sweetly and to relate sweetly. All in all, it seemed quite a culture shock after Kamyonistan.

Titania found herself immersed not only in the culture of the Middle East but also in the more rarefied culture of an international school abroad. She quickly found herself involved in social groups who gathered to play tennis, swim, make music, drink sundowners by the pool or make barbecues. These in turn morphed into committees to organise an autumn fair and a variety of future Christmas events.

At the end of the second week, she took a taxi to Kamyonistan to see the boys. 'You'll have to teach me how to ask for this place in Arabic,' she told Nuri. 'The taxi driver hadn't a clue how to get here. In the end, I made him stop and ask a lorry driver.'

'You did the right thing, then,' Ro laughed. 'How's it going at the…?' Ro paused, unable to think of the right word.

'Chalk face,' Titania filled in for him.

'Chalk face?' Ro sounded puzzled. Titania remembered that schools didn't use chalk any more. Ro probably hadn't seen a stick of chalk since the infants' classes. How things had changed!

'It's going well at the moment. Mind you, the honeymoon period isn't over yet. An old campaigner like me knows to wait and see how it all works out. By the way, I'm having a little drinks party in my apartment on Saturday. It would be lovely to have you there, but I'll understand if you don't want to go traipsing halfway across Damascus to get to it.'

'We're working, aren't we?' Nuri said. 'That's the day lots of trucks are arriving from the Gulf, and also the day we will receive that Iranian convoy.'

'Not another one!' Titania said, aghast. 'Have you heard the news of an invasion threat? Several of our staff have said they'll leave if there's any sign of hostility.'

'Most people here think it's all hot air,' Ro said. 'I wouldn't worry about it.'

'You'll have the Three Musketeers with you soon,' Titania said. 'I rang Bingo last night to make sure my house is still in one piece. He said they were loading together in Milton Keynes during today and tomorrow.'

'They'll be here towards the end of next week, then,' Ro said. He topped her *shay* glass up.

'I like what you've done with your garden,' Titania said. She took in the chairs, the makeshift table and the fire, to which Nuri constantly attended. Titania wondered, not for the first time, what would become of the pair, the couple even. What would they be doing at her age? Where would they be? Would they be together, still? She would be over a hundred by then, so she may never find out, she thought.

Ro broke her reverie with, 'Titania, do you think we just chase the illusion of paradise?'

'Probably,' she said. 'Does it matter whether it's an illusion or not?'

'I want the real thing!' Ro said.

'How would anyone know what "real" paradise was?' Titania asked.

'You would know by the feel of it,' said Ro.

'Then trust your intuition and enjoy paradise as and when it manifests itself,' answered Titania.

Ro's phone went and he answered it. 'Brilliant. Thanks. I'll tell her now.' He turned to Titania. 'Mehmet says we've all to go and eat at the Janna, and afterwards he'll drive you home because he's got some meat to pick up in Damascus.'

Snowflakes floated sedately in the air as three British-registered trucks in Kamyonistan Long-Haul Services colours left the customs area at Ruse. They headed south towards the mountains of Bulgaria, with Bingo at the head. His CB radio crackled and Eric's voice said, 'Bingo, got your ears on, breaker?'

'Yes, mate.'

'Are we going up Shipka or are we going up Little Shipka?'

'Little Shipka?'

'You know, Republic Pateka,' Eric said.

'I don't mind. They like us to go up Shipka because it's the old TIR route,' Bingo said.

'I'm only a boy at the job,' Jumbo's voice cut in, 'but if this snow sets in, we don't want to be going up Shipka. It's a lot higher than the other one.'

'We'll go Republic, then,' Bingo replied. Even as he replaced the microphone, the snowflakes began to blow across the windscreen in flurries. The traffic was light and they made steady progress on the two-way road. An hour later, the snow was driving hard into their faces, leaving clusters of big flakes on the windscreens. Gradually, the road surface disappeared under a white blanket. In the early afternoon, as they began to climb the foothills of the mountain, Bingo saw brake lights in front of him, then hazard lights and a distant queue of lorries standing in the road. He came to rest behind a Turkish tilt.

The three drivers walked up the line a little way after locking their cabs. Most of the drivers ahead were fitting snow chains. 'The police sometimes stop you going up if you haven't got them,' Jumbo said. They sauntered back through the deepening snow, and with great reluctance pulled out their snow chains. Diesel exhaust drifted down to them from the idling engines. Most drivers had put their night heaters on and were afraid to turn the engines off.

Two hours later, the queue began to move, one lorry length at a time. They edged round a Romanian truck that had slid halfway off the road. Eventually they came to a policeman who was sending lorries up the mountain one at a time and checking that the tyres had chains. In slow motion, the line of wagons ascended the forested mountain road through the snow-filled gloom of an early winter's afternoon. At the top, everything was jammed up. Eric was despatched to undertake a recce. When he arrived back, Bingo and Jumbo were sipping Turkish *chai* with the driver who had preceded them up the mountain.

'It's chocka down there,' Eric said. 'We're at the very summit. After this, the road falls sharply away and the hill's full of lorries pointing in all directions. It's absolute chaos down there. We won't be going anywhere tonight. I reckon we should get a bit of *kamyon gulash* on the go.'

'We'll be in trouble if this lot freezes,' Bingo said. 'I had this in Turkey a couple of years ago. It was like driving down a glacier full of parked lorries. Murder, it was.'

'We should come Italy–Greece when the weather's bad,' Eric said.

'What's the point? The Greek ferry costs a fortune and you can still get stuck in Greek snow. I was four days at Komotini a while back,' Jumbo said.

They cooked a hurried meal at Jumbo's trailer box, consisting of finely chopped potatoes and some tinned meat and vegetables, to which Bingo added fresh garlic. They washed it down with English-style tea and repaired to their cabs for warmth. Eric listened to the eerie, beautiful sound of a Bulgarian women's folk choir on Radio Sofia. In the dark, the snow stopped but the muffled rumble of idling diesels continued.

Bright sunlight smudged the icy road surface with yellow next morning. One by one, the southbound lorries edged their way over the summit and crept down the treacherous descent past the mirrors and doors of the northbound queue. The slightest error of judgement on the brake pedal or steering wheel would have brought the whole thing to a catastrophic halt, resulting in road closure. Picking their way round the oncoming lorries, the three drivers made it to the bottom and set off towards the Turkish border at Kapikule. Here, they spent the following evening working their way round the various windows and offices to get the TIR carnets stamped and pay the many and various levies. It took so long that in the end they decided to call it a day, go through the border and park in one of the TIR parks just outside.

Ro and Nuri attended Friday prayers in the drivers' mosque. Very few people were there and a bitterly cold wind swept off the mountain into the courtyard. Afterwards they spoke a little with the kindly imam before going to the compound gate, where they were picked up by Titania's friend, Doreen, who had a small Fiat. The four of them travelled into Damascus to see the stunning Umayyad Mosque. In all the time that Ro and Nuri had been associated with Kamyonistan, they had never been into Damascus to see this extraordinary building. They paced about in it with a sense of serene awe. Even Nuri, despite his background, had never set foot in a big, congregational mosque. Although he was Egyptian, he had never been to Cairo, so he had never seen the fabulous mosques of his own capital city, either. They went for coffee afterwards and Doreen promised to take them to see the old medina the following weekend. In return, she said, she would like to see the camels.

When they returned to Kamyonistan, Doreen was very excited

about the camels. 'I hadn't realised you had a baby one too. Titania, the children would love this. Let's get Mohammed to bring my class up here in the minibus to see them! The head will be fine with that if there are two of us with them.'

So it was arranged and the following Tuesday, Nuri found himself fielding the unpredictable questions of seven-year-olds as they ran their soft hands through the hair of the baby camel. 'Do they lay eggs?' one asked, and Nuri thought of Azhar and his apparently laid egg. Another child presented Nuri with a melon he had brought in that morning for the nature table but was finding too cumbersome to carry about.

When Ro came in that evening, he saw the great melon sitting in the middle of the table. 'What's that doing there?' he asked Nuri.

'It's a camel's egg,' Nuri replied.

'Oh,' Ro said. 'Had a good day?'

'I keep thinking about my parents,' Nuri said. 'I'm a bit worried about them. They may be frightened for me. No one in the family knows where I am. Even though I'm a bit of an outcast, I don't think any of them would want to see me come to any harm. The only reason I'm not with them, after all, is because they're in Saudi, and not because we can't stand each other. Mind you, they won't be pleased to know I'm back with you.'

'I wish I was allowed in Saudi, Nuri; I'd go with you to find them,' Ro said.

'But you are allowed,' said Nuri.

'I'm not. Bingo said they don't accept tourists and even lorry drivers can only go in by invitation,' Ro said, adamantly.

'That was before you were a Muslim, silly!' Nuri exclaimed. 'You can go in now, if you are doing hajj at Mecca.'

'Blimey! We could go on a hajj and then go and find your family. Where do they live?'

'They're Bedu; they might be anywhere,' Nuri said.

'Saudi's huge, though, isn't it? It'd be like looking for a needle in a haystack!' Ro said.

'Somebody in Nuweiba might know, if my grandfather's kept contact with them,' Nuri said doubtfully.

'So we go to Sinai, spend for ever trying to find someone who might have kept contact with your grandfather, then go on a pilgrimage to Mecca – and then start combing the desert for a family, the whereabouts of whom we don't know and who may greet us with hostility,' Ro said, dismissively.

'It was just a thought,' Nuri said. 'Anyway, we haven't got the money, and there'd be no one to look after the camels.'

'Unless you went on your own,' Ro said. 'That way I could keep the *felous* rolling in and take care of the camels. Then you wouldn't have to muck about doing a pilgrimage in Mecca because you're an Arab and don't have to prove anything. You could go straight in and start your search. You'd have to do your homework in Sinai first, though. Start your search from here on that laptop of yours.'

'I don't know...' Nuri began.

'Be confident, Nuri. You're coming up for eighteen, you can communicate, use a computer, speak languages, sort problems out intelligently and still ride a camel! You're not exactly a novice in life,' Ro said.

'I'll think about it,' Nuri replied uneasily.

Ro felt a sense of rising panic inside him. It would be unbearable without Nuri, but he knew that he shouldn't let his feelings of insecurity prevent Nuri from attempting his mission.

Snowbound

An icy draught blew in from the veranda. Ro sat with Azhar on his lap while Aysha laid tables for lunch. Nuri pushed the door open and closed it firmly behind him. His *shamagh* was pulled tightly round his head to keep out the wind. Absent-mindedly, Ro pressed his lips to the soft, warm, feathery back of Azhar's little head and let his hands dance a little, for his index fingers were gripped by tiny hands on both sides. Nuri threw his paperwork on the table. He smelt of camel. Mehmet entered, blowing into his hands. 'There's grilled fish today if you want it,' he said.

'*Samak meshwi*? Good-oh, I'll have some of that,' Nuri said.

'Make that two please,' said Ro. 'It's getting very cold out there. The wind is the worst.'

'The baby's suffering,' Nuri said. 'I've had to put him back in the shelter.'

Aysha lifted the other baby off Ro's lap and took him into the kitchen. 'The three drivers should be here by now,' Ro commented.

'There's been snow in Turkey,' Nuri said. 'They're in Jeddah!'

'Who are in Jeddah? Bingo, Jumbo and Eric?' Ro asked, surprised.

'No, my family,' Nuri said. 'I found a contact on the Net and did a bit of asking around. They've all settled on the outskirts of Jeddah.'

'You could fly there from Damascus Airport!' Ro said, encouragingly.

'Can we afford it?' Nuri asked.

'We can save up!' said Ro.

Fahmy pushed into the room and ordered coffee. 'Ro, could you move those Iranian trailers onto the concrete for me after lunch? It's snowing in Aleppo, and if it comes down this way, I don't want them stuck where we can't pull them out.'

'OK. Any news of the English lorries?' Ro asked.

'Tomorrow. That's if the snow doesn't stop them,' Fahmy said. He blew on his coffee. 'That fish smells good. I think I'll join you!'

When the drivers referred to by Titania as 'the Three Musketeers' finally appeared through the Islamic gates of Kamyonistan truck stop, snow was being blown across the harsh mountain landscape by a fiercely cold wind. The ground was a whitey-brown colour and the sides of parked trucks were becoming caked with snow. Traffic within the transport zone was busy.

Word got to Ro and Nuri that their friends had arrived. They found them at lunch time, huddled round the solid fuel-burning stove in the Janna, surrounded by woolly hatted drivers clutching *shay* glasses and cigarettes.

'Good trip down?' Ro asked, breezily.

'No, bloody awful!' Jumbo answered cheerfully. 'Snow since leaving Romania, a puncture, a broken snow chain and a wagon that eats fuses.'

'A good trip, all told,' Eric contradicted. 'No wrecks, no blown-up engines, no disintegrating gearboxes and no deaths that we've noticed.'

'Jumbo was dead on Wednesday,' Bingo put in, 'but on Thursday he rose again. Touch of the trots.'

'Touch of the Efes, you mean,' Eric said, referring to a Turkish beer. 'Anyway, what news at this end, young man?'

'Life goes on. Listen, Nuri says you won't get cleared today, so you won't be tipping until tomorrow afternoon at the very earliest. Titania wants us to go down to her flat and have a drink with her. Mehmet says he'll run us all down there after lunch as he has provisions to buy, and in any case, Amoun wants to get some cough mixture for Aysha.'

'Good plan!' Jumbo said, rubbing his hands. 'Will there be beer? I love beer!'

Following a leisurely lunch, Bingo, Jumbo, Eric, Ro and Amoun squeezed into Mehmet's capacious but ancient Peugeot. The snow had settled in many places and drifts were forming. 'It's turning into a blizzard,' Jumbo observed. 'I hope we can get back up the mountain again tonight. Where are you going, Mehmet? The road's thataway!'

'I'm taking the new access road,' Mehmet said. 'It's not open yet but it's quicker.' They hit a speed ramp and the passengers nearly went through the roof.

'Bloody hell, mate!' Jumbo exclaimed.

'I know!' Mehmet said, resignedly. 'I don't think much of those speed ramps either: if anything, they slow you down!'

At Titania's apartment, they were met by the *bawaab* who looked after the block. He shook their hands and gave a note to Mehmet, who passed it on to Bingo. It was handwritten.

Dear Everybody,

Can't wait to see you all. The doorkeeper will let you in with my spare key. The kitchen is yours but there's no booze yet, I'm afraid. That's why I'm late. I've gone to Doreen's to find out where the nearest equivalent to an off-licence is. The plan is that she will bring me back, suitably laden, in her car. See you soon. Take care.

Titania

'Bless her! She shouldn't be going to all this trouble; we've only come for tea,' Eric said.

'She must think we're all alchies,' Jumbo protested.

'So?' Eric commented.

'I'll go and get my provisions,' said Mehmet, 'and return in two or three hours' time. You might as well stay here and "party", Amoun. I can get your cough medicine.'

The remaining five entered the apartment and made themselves at home. Bingo put the kettle on and they stood at the large window that gave onto a balcony, watching the snow deepen at an alarming rate. 'We'll have to be careful we don't get snowed up here,' Jumbo said. 'We don't want to starve!'

'Allah will provide,' Ro said, automatically.

'No, he won't!' Bingo said, irritably. 'He doesn't provide for Muslims so he certainly isn't going to provide for us. God is not responsible for providing for us. Neither God nor the universe is responsible for feeding us, curing our mental illnesses, making us give up drugs or finding us a job! It's all down to us, mate.'

'Blimey, Bingo, the lad only said that Allah will provide,' Jumbo said, calmly.

'I know, but I'm sick of hearing about God or "the universe" being there to bail us out. If we don't take full responsibility for ourselves, we're never going to sort out our problems. *God* is not responsible for our behaviour, our income, our health or our sanity: *we* are. The sooner we come to terms with being entirely responsible for ourselves, our thoughts, our words, our actions and the consequences of them, the better.'

'God's a dangerous illusion, then?' Ro said.

'God's a serious cop-out,' Bingo said. 'He's even used as an accident insurance waiver in parts of the Middle East. How can you call a country struggling into the twenty-first century a "developing country" if its citizens think that political appointments and railway disasters are the will of God? Belief in God discourages responsibility. Look at Iraq… The first mistake the coalition made was to attack Iraq. Their second mistake was to assume that the Iraqis would take responsibility for their country and their future. Instead, they are all destroying each other in the name of God. America's not able to take responsibility for them because it believes that its own version of God will sanction their vengeful and immoral invasions. It is insanity to believe in God.'

'Well, I'm glad you got that off your chest,' Jumbo said with gentle sarcasm.

'Yes, Bingo,' said Eric with a smirk, 'thank you for sharing.'

Jumbo giggled. Eric joined in; Ro did too. Even Bingo was able to laugh at himself in the end. 'Piss-taking bastards!' he muttered.

Amoun was totally bewildered; firstly by the very suggestion that God might not exist, secondly by Bingo's temerity in daring to suggest it, thirdly by the lack of seriousness with which Bingo's words were taken, and fourthly by the humour with which his diatribe was received.

It was almost dark when Ro's phone rang. 'It's Titania,' he told them after the call. 'She says that she is snowed in at Doreen's. We've to make ourselves at home, and there is plenty in the fridge.'

'We'd better get back,' said Jumbo, looking alarmed. He went downstairs with Amoun to talk to the *bawaab* and examine the street. They returned covered in snow.

'It's too late,' Jumbo announced miserably. 'The street's full of snow and abandoned cars. The doorkeeper told Amoun that no taxis are running and that the main road to Homs is closed.'

They turned on the television, which showed snowploughs clearing runways at the airport and tense discussions between world leaders about the volatility of the region.

A knock on the door surprised them. It was Mehmet, soaked through, carrying two large shopping bags. 'I had to leave the rest in the car,' he said. 'I don't expect we'll see any of it again. I've walked miles and miles.' Bingo found some towels and ran a hot shower. Eric put the kettle on. Bingo started to pull food out of the fridge. The windows steamed up. Elderly radiators supplied constant heat.

When Mehmet emerged, glowing, from the bathroom, he said, 'I'm worried about the restaurant and all those stranded drivers.'

'Don't worry about them,' Ro said. 'Amoun and I have just spoken to Nuri and Aysha. They've locked up the Janna and taken Azhar with them to stay with Kamal in his nice warm apartment.'

'Couldn't she have kept the place going at tickover?' Mehmet asked.

'She was going to, but a group of Polish and Lithuanian drivers had hit the bottle and she could see that they didn't know when to stop,' Ro said.

'They've got the drivers' suq,' Amoun said. 'They can still feed themselves. In any case, they all carry food, especially in winter.'

Ro's phone rang again. 'Hello?' he said. 'Hello... hello? Damn. The card's run out.'

After their meal, the six men sat at the table and looked at one another. 'Shame there's no beer,' Jumbo said.

'You can live without beer,' Bingo answered. 'We can create our own happiness without it.'

'I don't like not being able to talk to Nuri,' Ro said. 'Bloody phone!'

'Aha!' Bingo said. 'Do you remember when we talked about the way in which we were all probably addicted to Kamyonistan in general and something else in particular?'

'Here we go!' Eric sighed.

'No, listen. We are all separated from Kamyonistan by the snow, so we've got to live without it for now. Then, if you go round the table: I am separated from the Middle-East run; Ro is separated from Nuri; Amoun is separated from Azhar; Jumbo is separated from his beer; Mehmet is separated from his beloved restaurant; and Eric is separated from any lorries. Even Titania, though absent, is separated from the community. Nuri may even be separated from the camels!'

'I hope not,' said Ro. 'The little one might die.'

'Don't you see, though, we are all faced with separation from Kamyonistan, to which I contended that we were addicted; and from the personal, subsidiary addictions too!' Bingo said, triumphantly.

'Well, that's jolly, isn't it?' Eric said. Jumbo swiped him playfully round the head. 'Hit me again: I can still hear him!' Eric said.

'So, are we going to sit here and be victims?' Bingo asked. 'Are we going to wait until God makes it all right again? Are we going to resign ourselves to inevitable unhappiness until our Nuris, beers, Azhars, lorries, restaurants and Middle-East runs are duly restored to us? Or are we going to generate our own happiness using our own inner resourses?'

'Doesn't that miss the point a little?' Eric countered. 'I mean, if we were to sit here long enough, wouldn't we simply replace the old so-called addictions with new ones? Mehmet might become a telly addict, Ro might become addicted to Amoun, Jumbo might take up fags again and become addicted to tobacco, and you might replace your addiction to the Middle-East run with an addiction to the city of Damascus.'

'But those are all external things,' Bingo said. 'There has to be something from within. We should be able to draw upon the inviolable place inside us, wherein lies the potential for paradise.' Ro nodded in silent recognition.

'Why invalidate external life?' said Eric. 'If I lived on a desert island with no prospect of ever seeing a lorry again for the rest of my life, I would spend the first year fondly remembering them, then I would become happily obsessed with jellyfish, especially the lesser Mediterranean Twin-Splitting jellyfish.' Jumbo began to laugh again and they adjourned to the comfy chairs. Discussion broke out about the possible sleeping arrangements. Mehmet, not averse to his suggested role as plausible telly addict, switched on the television. The picture was poor. He turned the sound down. Then the lights went out. After a good deal of groping and giggling in the pitch dark they all found corners in which to curl up under coats and blankets.

Ro woke up to a rushing sound. He opened his eyes; it was daylight. His neck was stiff and aching from a draught that had assailed him throughout the night. An intensely bright light flickered round the room, followed by an immense crash of thunder. He tottered to the window. It was raining very heavily. Some of the snow had already been washed away. Another crash of thunder woke the others. Ro put the kettle on. 'Is this what's called a "storm in a teacup" in English?' Amoun asked.

'Yes.' Ro giggled.

'We'll have breakfast,' Bingo announced. 'Then we'd better see if we can find that car of yours, Mehmet. If the weather holds off, maybe we can entertain Titania and her chum in good old addictive Kamyonistan!'

'Well, it's still only November,' Eric said. 'We could easily be sitting in the sun on the veranda tomorrow afternoon!'

Titania

Mehmet wiped the inside of the windscreen with his wet sleeve as he drove. His other hand moved in sympathy on the steering wheel so that the car swerved about on the flooded road. 'So, as I understand it, Bingo,' he was saying, 'you think God's an illusion, or a delusion, and Eric is saying, "So what? It doesn't matter." Am I right?'

'Yes,' Bingo said.

'As a Muslim, I do think it matters, of course. God is the basis of everything in the world. If you're not with him, you're against him,' Mehmet said.

'How can I be against something I don't believe to exist?' Bingo asked. The car slowed suddenly, then stopped. A police officer leaned in through the driver's open door and carefully surveyed the soaking mass of humanity within.

Mehmet explained his purpose and the officer waved them on. Mehmet put the car into gear and started up the mountain. 'Apparently, the snow is still bad further up,' he said. 'It's rained on Damascus but not up here.'

He followed the ruts in the increasingly difficult road. It had stopped snowing. They arrived at the point at which the new access road joined the main road, after which the main road was full of snow. The orange beacons of snowploughs could be seen in the distance. Mehmet pulled onto the access road and they all got out, each carrying a bag of Mehmet's provisions. Leaving the car, they began to trudge through the snow to Kamyonistan.

Amoun went to find Aysha while Mehmet and the drivers lit the stoves and got the Janna up and running. By mid-afternoon, the smell of food, wet drivers and woodsmoke filled the air. 'Your loads are cleared,' Nuri announced above the din of Arabian music, handing the three English drivers their papers.

'But you can't go and tip yet because of the snow,' Kamal said.

'Well, get it cleared!' Jumbo urged. 'Before we all go bankrupt!'

'How?' Kamal said lamely. He shot a glance at Fahmy, who had just sat down with a glass of Turkish raki.

'Do you mean to say that you haven't got a snowplough?' Bingo asked, menacingly.

'The military have always cleared Kamyonistan for us,' Fahmy said. 'Now that they've pulled out, we've nothing.'

'It's quite comforting to know that this place is no longer of any strategic importance, then, isn't it!' Eric said with enthusiasm, thinking of the rocket attack.

'But Fahmy, your business is on a mountain!' Bingo persisted. 'With all that equipment for lifting and moving containers and loads, I would have thought that the early acquisition of a snowplough would have been an obvious choice!'

'We inherited the container kit when we took over. There hasn't been money for a snowplough,' Fahmy said, lamely.

'No one thought of it, you mean,' Bingo said.

'The snow won't last,' said Fahmy.

'If I were the director of this company, I'd get my wellies on and go and talk to one of those snowplough drivers out there in the main road – make him an offer he couldn't refuse. This site should have a resident snowplough on it, not just at KLHS, but one at the disposal of the whole zone community as well,' Bingo said. 'All you need is one of your old shunters, a removable ballast box and a detachable plough for the front.'

'I don't know what's got into Bingo this trip,' Eric said. Turning to Bingo, he said, 'If you're going to be a crosspatch, I'm going to eat at another table.' Jumbo began to laugh. Bingo looked at Jumbo and said, 'Can you think of anything this place needs more than a snowplough?'

'Yes,' Jumbo said, 'more beer!'

Nuri sat down next to Ro. 'How's our baby holding up against this weather?' Ro asked.

'They're both happy enough in that shelter,' Nuri said. 'I've booked a flight to Jeddah.'

'What?'

'I got Maryam in the office to do it for me online. It's booked and paid for,' Nuri said.

'Blimey, that was quick! When are you going?'

'Monday. Aren't you going to ask me how much it cost?'

'No. If I had parents alive to visit, I wouldn't expect anyone else to count the cost of a visit to see them,' Ro replied.

'Come on, men,' Bingo said suddenly, getting up. 'Let's go and run those lorries up for an hour or so. Then we'll come back and drink lots of beer.'

Jumbo quaffed the dregs of his drink and followed Bingo and Eric outside. It was nearly dark and snowing heavily. 'No good fighting nature, is it?' Bingo commented.

When Titania appeared at the Janna in the early evening, no one could quite believe it. 'It's impossible!' Bingo slurred, 'You cannot have come through all that snow!'

'Nobody told me it was still snowing on the mountain,' Titania said. 'The policeman who turned my taxi round took pity on me and put me in a snowplough.'

'You came here in a snowplough?' Bingo said, incredulously. 'I hope it was the new one I told Fahmy to order. Here, let me get you a drink. Do you want a crig of basps?'

'What are you saying, Bingo? This isn't a pub: they don't sell crisps here!' Titania chuckled. 'I've never seen you pissed before. What it all about?'

'Aysha's having a baby,' Eric said quickly. 'She announced it this evening. We're celebrating, aren't we, Bingo?'

'Absolutely. I shouldn't be surprised if she didn't have a baby!' Bingo replied. Jumbo exploded with laughter. 'That would be a turn-up for the bloody books, wouldn't it? Aysha having a baby!' he cackled. 'What do you think she'll have?'

'I reckon she'll have a baby,' Eric said. Bingo roared. Jumbo shook until tears coursed down his cheeks. 'What else did you think she would have, then?' he howled.

Mehmet took Titania's arm. 'It'll be cold in that cab tonight, and none too pleasant, I imagine. Stay upstairs with me; I've got a spare room. Aysha can make up a bed for you.'

'That's very gallant of you. I hope your intentions are honourable!'

'As honourable as you want them to be, madam,' answered Mehmet, who was probably twenty years her junior.

'I shouldn't want to be put to bed by a man who turned out to be a rotter!' Titania said. Eric, who overheard this, began to laugh anew. Bingo, who thought Eric was laughing afresh at the baby business, cried, 'I'll lay odds that Aysha's child will be a baby!' and collapsed in uncontrollable mirth again.

Mehmet handed Titania a gin and tonic. 'That's a big one!' she cried. Mehmet gave her a look and she added quickly, 'I mean, I hope you're not trying to get me tipsy. I didn't even know you had gin here.'

'We didn't. I bought it especially for you, when we went for the provisions,' Mehmet said.

'Don't tell Jumbo that! He wasn't very impressed about having a "dry" night in Damascus.' Titania giggled. She chinked glasses with Mehmet and he gave her a conspiratorial wink.

Nuri and Ro returned to the cabins to try and coax enough heat out of the stoves to make the night bearable. They were determined to stick it out in the cabin rather than stay with Kamal. After all, this was not the first time they had been snowed up in Kamyonistan.

It had stopped snowing in the night and the clouds had blown over. This resulted in a very cold but sunny morning. Frost glittered brightly on the snow. Aysha remained in bed with morning sickness, as did Bingo. Titania undertook Aysha's tasks with such happy alacrity that Amoun began to wonder if she had been at the bottle before breakfast. He could have sworn that he saw Mehmet tickle her when he turned away from looking out of the window, but he put it down to snow blindness. The cock crowed in the snow outside. Mehmet turned on the music. Ro and Nuri finished their breakfasts and trudged through the snow, without either shunter or camel, to report for duty.

They found an army of men and boys shovelling snow in the yard. Some of them had evidently been there for hours. They recognised two of the shoeshine boys, some workshop boys, several drivers, office staff, and a host of odd-job workers who hung around the zone in hope of casual employment. Kamal was there in a red woolly hat looking radiant with exertion. The day, it seemed, would be spent clearing snow. Finally, the essential loading bays were cleared and they all went for lunch.

Titania

Ro and Nuri were surprised to find Titania serving meals as if she'd been born to it. Jumbo, still the worse for wear from the night before, was singing 'All Things Bright and Beautiful' in the echoing gents at the top of his voice. Eric was eating his lunch and Bingo was conspicuously absent.

'Dead to the world, mate!' Eric commented. 'We'll tip ours this afternoon. I'll pull Bingo's unit out from under his trailer. Ro, if you can connect your shunter to it, perhaps you could tip it for him. Will they do all three trailers at once, Nuri?'

'Yes. They've just realised that these loads are urgent!' Nuri said.

Later, Ro wound Bingo's trailer legs down while Eric built the air up. Eric then began to ease Bingo's DAF forward. It began to slip. He engaged the diff-lock. The wheels bit and the unit slid out. He parked the DAF near the Janna and left the engine running on fast tickover and the night heater running. Then the three lorries made their way through the snow to the loading bays in the KLHS yard.

The following day, the weather warmed up considerably. A gang of six went to rescue Mehmet's car, and Titania was taken back to her apartment. When Mehmet returned to Kamyonistan, he discovered that Titania had left her scarf in the kitchen. He announced his intention to take it down to her the following evening. Amoun shared his suspicions with the boys, who were highly amused. The Three Musketeers, meanwhile, awaited news of their reloads with patience, fortitude and moderate sobriety.

Caravanserai

Amoun ran into the restaurant, nearly knocking over Ro, who was talking to Nuri on his mobile phone. 'Quick!' Amoun shouted. 'Someone's in Bingo's cab!'

Everyone rushed to the door. A man in blue dungarees and lumber jacket was climbing into a KLHS-liveried truck. 'It's him! That's the man!' Amoun shouted.

Eric ran out onto the veranda. 'Careful, Eric!' Jumbo called. 'He's Russian. They're generally well tooled up. They carry guns in Russia.'

Eric made for his lorry. Bingo began to trot towards the open door of his cab. The Russian was having trouble getting the air pressure up on his 6 x 6 Tatra. 'Run to the gate and alert the police,' Jumbo said to Amoun. Ro gave a running commentary to Nuri, who in turn announced that the director, Mustafa, would be over immediately. Eric's lorry began to roll and he turned it towards the main gate. The Russian tilt followed. Amoun reached the gate just before Eric. Eric slewed the truck round at the last minute, before jackknifing it in reverse to block the entrance entirely. When the Russian ran to confront Eric, he was immediately joined by the duty policeman, the gate man and Amoun. Seconds later, Jumbo and Mehmet pulled up in the old Peugeot. The policeman and the gate man held the Russian, while they waited for Bingo to arrive.

'Just my passport and £500 sterling,' he announced, panting.

'Fuel cards?' asked Jumbo.

'No, they're safe.' The Tatra was searched. Then the driver was searched and the stolen items were found in his pockets. At that moment a car pulled up and Mustafa, the director of KLHS, climbed out with Nuri and Fahmy. The policeman apprised him of the situation, and Mustafa then made three telephone calls. Finally, he gave instructions to the policeman and the gate man, who took the Russian into the gatehouse in handcuffs.

'So!' he said turning to Bingo. 'Well done, everybody, for apprehending him. We will impound his truck. He will be tried in Damascus tomorrow, then he will be taken to the border and his passport will be marked to the effect that re-entry is not permitted. If he can afford it, he will be allowed to fly to Moscow. Either way, he's barred.'

'Blimey!' Eric said. 'I wish the European countries would do that.'

'They can't,' said Jumbo. 'There are no border controls any more.'

'Beats chopping off their hands,' smiled Bingo.

'Now then,' Mustafa said. 'If any of you can work out how to drive this Czech-built truck, perhaps you would park it over by the offices for me. Ro, you can put the trailer back on bay number six, and we'll get it unloaded again. Then stick the trailer in the parking compound somewhere, we might be able to use that later. Take an extra hour for lunch.'

Mehmet plonked his *shay* glass back on the table. 'For all your talk of taking responsibility for the things we say, Bingo, you still insist on freedom of speech,' he said.

'The two are reconcilable,' Bingo said. 'They are not mutually exclusive. Taking a critical look at the Muslim ideal is not the same as attacking Muslims.'

'It is, if they feel aggrieved by the critical looking,' Mehmet answered.

'You have to remember that if we're triggered by what people say, we still own the feelings that are triggered, so they are our responsibility,' Bingo said.

'If you attack me verbally and I feel pain, I will hold you responsible for the pain,' Mehmet said.

'Agreed,' said Bingo, 'but if I attack an idea and you then take it personally, you are no longer in a position to hold me responsible, because I attacked the idea and not you personally.'

'Isn't it a case of ensuring that we use language that minimises the risk of someone perceiving attack where none is intended?' Eric asked.

'It's more than that,' Mehmet answered. 'If you understand the culture of Islam, you will realise that a Muslim takes all criticism of Islam personally – whether you, with your psychology-based mindset, like it or not. Asking several million Muslims to disassociate themselves personally from their religion is just plain unrealistic.'

Jumbo joined them. He opened a can of beer. 'I've just been listening to the news,' he said. 'Bush has announced the extension of sanctions against Syria as a result of threats to US national security, US foreign policy and the US economy.'

'Why?' Mehmet asked.

'He accuses Syria of supporting terrorism and pursuing weapons of mass destruction and missile programmes, including illicit nuclear cooperation with North Korea.'

'Added to the food shortages, that doesn't sound too good,' Mehmet said.

'God will provide,' Ro said, provocatively.

'You can cut that sort of talk out!' Jumbo laughed. 'You'll have Bingo back on his high horse in no time.'

'Come on, Ro, I've got to be back in the office,' Nuri said.

They sat in the shunter while the air built up, gazing through the dirty windscreen at the canopies of tilts whose bright colours merged into the pale patina of winter road grime from the waist down.

'I had a weird dream last night,' Nuri said. 'I dreamt that the architect, Ismail, brought me into the compound at night. The sky was midnight blue and the stars were really bright. All over the compound were little fires and makeshift tents. Hundreds of camels stood, knelt or lay near the encampments. Men wearing the robes and headgear of every tribe in the Middle East and beyond were tending the fires and camels. Ismail took me on a tour of the caravan, showing me precious stones, silks, metals, coffee, medicines and spices. Even though it was night-time, all the colours in the carpets, camel blankets and clothes seemed to be glowing. The frost sparkled under the stars.'

'Strewth!' Ro commented, letting the clutch out with a jerk. 'Next time you have that dream, take me with you. Perhaps unbeknown to anyone alive, this site really did have a caravanserai on it.'

'Perhaps,' Nuri said, distantly.

'You'll certainly get your fill of camels in Saudi,' Ro said. 'Fahmy's given me permission to go and see you off at the airport tomorrow, by the way.'

'Good,' Nuri smiled. 'I'm glad. I'm nervous about the trip.'

A day later, the three lorries had not been reloaded. Bingo and Jumbo were toying with newly opened beer cans in the Janna while Eric was retrieving his unit from the workshops. Mehmet arrived back with Ro and, to Bingo's surprise, Titania as well. Amoun sorted out some drinks and everyone sat down.

'Did Nuri get off all right?' Bingo asked.

'Yes. He was very nervous,' Ro said.

'He shouldn't be; he's an experienced traveller,' said Jumbo as Eric walked in.

'Got those fuses sorted yet?' Bingo called.

'Yes, mate! Mine's a pint,' Eric answered placidly. 'Nuri get off all right, Ro? I expect you're feeling a bit flat, aren't you?'

'Yes, thanks, on both counts,' Ro said.

'What's brought you up here so soon, Titania?' Bingo asked.

'Well, I'm terminating my contract at the end of the week,' Titania said.

'What? Jacking the job in already?' Jumbo muttered.

'I'm doing maternity cover, remember. The teacher concerned has had some bad luck; her child was stillborn. She has expressed a desire to return to work to take her mind off the tragedy. Contractually, I'm entitled to stay in post until February half-term. However, I feel for her and I don't need the work.'

'Blimey!' Bingo said. 'What are you going to do?'

'Well, I can't go home yet because there's some hairy-arsed lorry driver living in my house!' Titania laughed. Bingo chuckled obligingly.

'You've still got your flat in Damascus,' he said.

'No need,' Titania said. 'I'm going to stay here with Mehmet and help with the Janna, perhaps until Aysha's had her baby.'

Bingo's face lit up and he beamed at them both. 'I think that's a brilliant plan!' he said. 'Let's drink to it!'

'That's the most sensible suggestion you've made all week!' Jumbo laughed.

Fahmy walked in, wearing a donkey jacket and a woolly hat.

Bingo hailed him cheerfully. 'Come and have a celebratory raki with us!' he called.

'First you must come outside, Bingo,' Fahmy said, excitedly. 'I have something to show you.'

They all stood up and followed Fahmy outside. There, in the remnants of the snow, with its engine running and its spotlights blazing, was the 6 x 6 Tatra tractor unit with a newly fitted snowplough on the front. 'Perfect for the job!' Bingo laughed delightedly. 'Do you know anyone with a brand new DAF who we can persuade to nick my wallet?' he joked. Fahmy stopped the engine and joined them inside.

Ro closed his eyes as the voices babbled around him. He thought of Nuri's dream and he saw, as if through Nuri's eyes, the sparkling frost and the royal colours of carpets draped upon magnificent camels standing in the firelight. He wondered if the Greater Kamyonistan in Nuri's enchanted place would take on this historical guise, thus shedding its backdrop of Tatra snowploughs and grimy tilts. He wondered how different Nuri's Kamyonistan might have been from his, even before the dream. Then he wondered if their enchanted Kamyonistans would converge or diverge as time went by. He had always assumed that Nuri's was identical to his own. Now he was not so sure.

Aysha sat down next to him. 'Do you mind Titania coming?' he asked.

'I'm relieved,' she replied. 'It'll take the drudgery out of the job. I'll still have to do all the office work, because Titania doesn't know Arabic.'

'Excellent!' Ro said. 'Are you looking forward to the new baby?'

'It's a bit early to think too hard about that yet,' Aysha replied. 'Last time was pretty traumatic.'

'Ah yes!' said Ro. 'Are you going to get Amoun to deliver it for you again?'

'No!' Aysha laughed. 'This time I'll have a proper midwife, and no nonsense.'

'What are you going to call it?'

'We're not sure yet, but if it's a boy we'll probably call him Ismail, after the architect who created Kamyonistan.'

'That's very appropriate, considering that he'll be born here,' Ro remarked.

'If it's a girl, we might name her Titania,' Aysha whispered.

'Titania would be most honoured, I'm sure,' Ro smiled. He raised his glass. 'To the baby,' he said.

'To the baby,' she answered, patting her middle.

Mule Train

Ro had spent half the night helping to tranship wooden crates from containers that had come in a convoy from the docks at Latakia. They were moved onto military trucks that left in another convoy before daylight. He had been told to take the morning off to catch up on his sleep. After four hours, however, the daylight and noise of Kamyonistan woke him up and he got up. Wanting to do something a little different, he saddled up Nuri's camel and went for a wander down to look at the new access road. The camel was pleasant to ride so he cut across country round the south end of the transport zone and headed west. Although the sun was warm, a cold wind blew down the mountain from the north, and he wrapped his *shamagh* tightly round his head and face. Eventually he found a rocky track and followed it into the hills until Kamyonistan was out of sight. If he kept going in this direction, he thought, he would reach the Lebanese border in the end.

The sun rose higher. Another track joined his from higher up the mountain. Ro noticed fresh droppings on the ground and he hesitated. He considered going back. Then, as he rounded a steep bend, he saw a train of pack mules silhouetted against the sky between the hills ahead. Ro stopped and waited for them to vanish below the skyline. For a while he followed them, but he was uneasy. There was no guarantee that the men would be friendly. From time to time they reappeared against the misty, blue shapes of the distant hills. The track began to duck down steep dips and to twist round narrow summits. He wished he had brought some lunch with him. Then he realised that his mobile phone was still in the cabin. Without realising it he had nearly caught up with the mule train. Ro could see them clustered together under a tree not far ahead. They appeared not to have seen him. It was time to call it a day.

He turned the camel round and climbed back up the track the way he had come. Descending the other side he heard a shout. Then, without further warning a shot was fired. Scared, Ro dismounted, sliding down the standing camel Beduin-style. He crouched by the camel and waited. Then a dozen or so soldiers appeared on the other side of the cleft in the rocks. Slowly, he raised his hands and called, '*Selamu aleikum!*'

The soldiers approached with their rifles in front of them. He greeted them, and they shouted at him in rapid Arabic. He realised that his appearance, mode of transport and location would have failed to reveal that he was an Englishman. Ro needed to make it clear to them who he was, fast. In a mixture of Egyptian and Syrian Arabic, he declared who he was, where he had come from and why he was there. Suddenly, one of the soldiers shouted something at the others. One of them laughed. Then the others laughed too and they scrambled across the cleft to him, shaking his hand and thumping him on the back. 'Ro! Ro! How you are, English? Where's Nuri? New camel! Nice.'

It clicked. These were the boy soldiers who had played football with them two winters ago. They were grown-up now, and were clearly fully fledged soldiers. They would have remembered him only as a boy with a camel wearing a jalabiya and *shamagh*; so, ironically, had he been out on the mountain wearing a cagoul and a woolly hat, they would not have recognised him. The soldiers offered him cigarettes, which he graciously declined. One of them who spoke a little English said they were trying to apprehend some arms smugglers who used pack mules to cross the mountain border. Ro was glad he had turned round, and told them what he had seen. Immediately, they assigned two of their number to escort Ro to safety, while the rest set off at a run in pursuit of the mule train.

His escorts upbraided him for wandering about in the mountains alone. They warned him of mines and people who were best avoided. Just as they were nearing Kamyonistan, they heard distant gunfire in the hills. Ro shuddered. The young soldiers shook hands with him and ran off in the direction of their colleagues. He returned to his cabin, settled the camel and made himself a sandwich. Then, pocketing his phone, he went outside and checked the oil on the shunter before firing it up. His phone told him that it was 2.30.

'Why are you late for work, young man?' Fahmy said irritably.

'My camel and I encountered a mule train smuggling ordnance across the border and I alerted the army, who apprehended them while I retreated to safety,' Ro said.

'Have you been drinking?' Fahmy snapped.

'No, Fahmy! Listen…' It was only when Ro threatened to send for Amoun and Mahmout, who would vouch for the credibility of his story that Fahmy relented. 'All right, Lawrence of bloody Arabia, let's get some work done,' Fahmy said gruffly, trying to conceal his mirth from Ro.

'You were lucky not to get yourself shot!' Bingo said.

'After all that you've seen in these mountains, it must have occurred to you that it is dangerous to roam about outside the zone,' Mehmet said incredulously. Amoun wanted Ro to describe the soldiers to see which ones he remembered, and Mahmout confided that one of them had been hung like a pack mule. Ro asked him how he knew. He showed no sign of contrition and he greeted baby Azhar with, 'Hello! Have you been a good boy while Uncle Ro's been out there leading the Arab Revolt?'

'Stow it, Ro!' Bingo growled good-naturedly. 'Or I'll set Sykes and Picot on you!'

They laughed at Bingo's reference to the infamous pair from the English and French governments who deceived the Arabs of the Hejaz into believing that their revolt was successful, while in reality they planned to carve up the ailing Ottoman Empire between Britain, France and Russia.

'Ro!' Mehmet called. 'Come out and see these, will you!' Ro went into the little yard at the back of the restaurant. There were chicken coops and the general paraphernalia and mess of poultry lit by a naked bulb hanging from an upstairs window. 'Nuri's often shown an interest in keeping chickens. Can you take this lot off my hands? They're beginning to get in the way, and Titania keeps complaining that they're a health hazard, being so close to the restaurant kitchen.'

'Gladly,' Ro said. 'I'll do it tomorrow lunchtime if someone makes me a sandwich.'

'Be careful with that end one, Ro; there are two newly hatched chicks in there,' Mehmet said.

'What are they called?' Ro said.

'Chickens,' said Mehmet.

'No, what have you named them?'

'We don't name them, we just eat their eggs,' Mehmet said.

'Sykes and Picot!' Bingo called from the door.

'Done!' Ro laughed. 'Sykes and Picot they are. Nuri will be tickled when he sees these. I wonder how's he's getting on with his family.'

'Are their wings clipped?' Jumbo asked from inside. 'They'll just come back here again, otherwise.'

'Yes,' Mehmet said. 'It'll be nice to hear that damned cockerel calling from a distance instead of right under my window.'

'We'll help you with them, Ro!' Jumbo shouted. 'It'll only cost you a round!'

They adjourned to the dining room, which was filling up with drivers and cigarette smoke. The temperature had dropped sharply since sunset and there was talk of more snow. 'You could keep goats as well on that patch of land you've got there,' Jumbo said. 'You could do with a bit of a shed, though.'

'I've got one,' Ro said.

'I haven't noticed,' said Jumbo.

'When Fahmy told me to dump that empty Russian tilt in the compound I did exactly as I was told and parked in our domain,' Ro laughed.

'Not inside it?'

'Yes, I jackknifed it through the gate and jacked it again into the corner formed by the camel shelter and the wall,' Ro said.

'Blimey, Ro! Proper driver, then!' Jumbo cackled. 'Here Bingo, get a load of this; guess what Ro's done with that Ruski tilt...' He followed Bingo to the counter.

Ro sat quietly for a moment and pondered. Suddenly, he missed Nuri badly. Nuri would love all this messing about with chickens and tilts. He hoped that messing about with camels in Saudi would compensate. Aysha sat down with him. She looked pale.

'How's it going?' he asked.

'Not nearly as easily as the last one,' Aysha said. 'I didn't know I was carrying Azhar until the last minute.'

'You look a bit worn out,' Ro said.

'I've just been to the clinic. They were talking about an American-led invasion. I hope they're only scaremongering,' Aysha said.

'What did they say?'

'Well, for a start they said that all the Syrian borders may have to close.'

'When?'

'Who knows?'

'And the airport?'

'Who knows?'

Aysha got up and went into the kitchen. Ro frowned and went to order some food. He could hear Eric sounding off about DAF gearboxes. 'I don't know about your motor, Bingo, but on the old DAF 95s, if you lost low range, you could wire the range-change switch direct to the battery and bypass everything. The only thing was, you forfeited the built-in protection against accidentally engaging low range at speed. It certainly bailed you out if you were stuck in the middle of nowhere,' Eric said.

'Trouble is now, Eric,' Bingo replied, 'everything is done by computer electronics. If anything goes wrong, you need to plug a laptop into the works. Then all it does is to tell you it's shutting the system down until you buy new, expensive parts. We don't build lorries for long-haul work any more; not in Europe, anyway.'

Ro asked Mehmet for a bowl of goulash and plenty of bread. 'Do you think the old vet in the livestock compound would know where to find me a couple of kids?' he asked Mehmet.

'Children? What do you want them for?'

'No, young goats; I thought we might have a goat or two to run with the chickens and keep the camels in order,' Ro said.

Mehmet roared with laughter. 'Yes; try him!' he said.

Fish, Fog, Fire and Fear

Mehmet made a huge fish pie, which the disgruntled drivers tucked into while they waited for Ro to take his lunch break. It had begun to snow again and the drivers were frustrated by the lack of progress on the reload front. Workers were unable to get to Kamyonistan, so clothes were unfinished on the production line. Jumbo was able to load his trailer three-quarters full but the other two trailers remained empty. Ro arrived late and declined the fish pie. Between them all, they installed Ro's chickens and then went to the clothes factory to 'kick airse' as Eric put it in a mock-American accent.

Ro finished work early and made a serious attempt to get their domain in order while there was still some daylight. He fed the camels, watered the chickens and collected firewood for the stoves. Then he heaved their dwindling supply of hay into the Russian tilt, making a mental note to pick up some more from the livestock compound, which would now be filling up with sheep in preparation for Eid al Adhar. When the sunset call to prayer had faded and the light with it, he tried to rig up some outside lighting so that he could work outside on winter evenings. He planned to enter the broken minaret and install elevated lighting that would illuminate the domain when required. Realising that he would need help with this and a lot of wire, he swept out the neglected cabins instead.

The double-decked cabins were of a 45-foot ISO shipping container design, but having previously been used as site offices for Ismail's architectural consortium, they were well insulated and retained the warmth of the stoves admirably. The lower one comprised a shower-toilet and a kitchen divided by a small storeroom. Accessed by the external stairway, the upper cabin consisted of a bedroom and a sitting room that overlooked the TIR compound. The sitting room was rarely used in practice because the kitchen was the most lived-in space in the house.

Ismail had provided them with some basic furniture such as a table, two small push-together beds and some cupboards. Ro and Nuri had added garden chairs, which served both inside and out. The cooker and fridge had come with the cabins. Mehmet had donated rugs and blankets. The cabins, then, were not as spartan as they might have been. Firewood would have been a problem if Ro and Nuri had been less diligent in their surreptitious gleaning of scraps during each working day, resulting in both camel and shunter arriving home bristling with fuel.

Ro arrived at work the next morning to find Fahmy and Kamal absent, along with several other staff. Wishing to make good use of the time, he took an empty trailer round to the livestock compound in the worsening snow. The vet supplied him with hay under the arrangement made by Ismail, but he warned Ro that prices were soaring and that hay was in short supply because of the bad weather. Ro enquired about goats and received encouraging news of a possible pair within the zone.

Upon arrival at the Janna, Ro found the place deserted. After making brief enquiries he discovered that the fish pie had struck a gastronomic blow to Kamyonistan. Mehmet, Amoun, Bingo, Jumbo, Eric, Fahmy, Kamal, Mahmout and a host of others were fighting mild but debilitating food poisoning, each in their small corners. The only people left on the planet, it seemed to Ro, were Aysha and himself – along with Azhar, of course. Like district nurses, he and Aysha did the rounds to ensure that everyone was wrapped up warm and had easy access to a bowl.

Ro then returned to the shunters' rest room to find out what jobs ought to be done to keep the wheels turning.

Titania arrived the following evening in a taxi with all her belongings. She found the transport scene stagnant and the domestic scene catastrophic. Like a whirlwind, she did her own version of the district nurse's rounds, bustling everyone out of their torpor and galvanising them into action. She took Mehmet and Amoun to the suq for provisions, and by lunchtime the following day the Janna was back to normal. By then the snow had eased off, only to be replaced by a thick freezing fog.

The number of lorries arriving in the KLHS yard was reduced

Fish, Fog, Fire and Fear

to a trickle. Turkish drivers reported atrocious weather in Turkey and numerous road accidents on the road from Aleppo and Homs. Ro busied himself at home, digging over the soil where he planned to plant vegetables as soon as spring arrived. He wanted, as well, to create a home worth returning to, for Nuri. Each day, he asked in the office if Nuri had sent emails to anyone. He kept his phone charged at all times in case Nuri rang. The last text message he had received was from the runway at Damascus Airport.

'Don't worry too much, old thing,' Bingo said kindly, as they shared lunch in the fug of the Janna. 'If Nuri's family is stuck out in some Beduin encampment on the edge of Jeddah, he may not have access to computers. He may not have thought to buy a Saudi phonecard or it might have run out if he has. "No news is good news," they say.'

'But it's not like Nuri not to communicate,' Ro insisted.

'How do you know?' Bingo said. 'You've not been out of each other's sight since you were reunited all that time ago.'

'I hope you're right, Bingo,' Ro replied. 'Are you any good at rigging up patio lights?'

Bingo burst out laughing. 'Yes! Why?'

Ro's worst fears were allayed by the arrival of a small parcel. It was sitting on the counter in the Janna at lunchtime the following day. People were agog to know what it was. The parcel, covered in Saudi Arabian stamps, was addressed to Ro. When he opened it he found a wonderfully soft, camel-hair wrap. His joy at receiving it was nothing compared with his relief that Nuri was evidently alive and kicking.

Kamal entered, complaining that the fog was becoming thicker. Complimenting Ro on his wrap, he called to Bingo. 'Your load is ready,' he said, 'you can start this afternoon. The rest of Jumbo's load will be ready soon; they've started packing it. No news of Eric's, I'm afraid.'

The drivers knew that they wouldn't all finish loading at the same time. They were torn between the plan to leave as and when each trailer was loaded, which made sense economically, and their survival instincts to stick together during crisis and inclement weather. They chose the latter plan.

'Turkey can be a swine in winter,' Jumbo said. 'We'll slow each other down, but we'll keep each other alive.'

Ro was woken in the night by the wail of sirens. At first he thought that their fears of an invasion had been realised. Then he recognised the distinctive wail of fire engines. He went to the window. Through the fog he could just discern an orange glow behind the gates of the parking compound. He got dressed and went outside. There were people running; he could hear their footfalls. Picking his way among the parked lorries, he made his way through the gate and out into the service road and followed the glow. He found a number of familiar faces gazing forlornly at the burning wreckage of what had, that afternoon, been the clothes factory that exported its products to the UK.

'That's Eric's load and the rest of Jumbo's gone up in smoke,' Bingo said, bitterly.

'More than that, mate,' Jumbo said. 'That's our hopes for the Middle-East run gone up in smoke! There's nothing else that comes out of here for Blighty.'

'You're right there,' said Eric. 'I shall have to pick up groupage in Italy on the way home. We'll be doing bloody containers round the M25 in the new year at this rate.'

After a while, the fog began to pale and they all realised that it must be dawn. They adjourned to the Janna, where Amoun stoked the stoves and Titania helped Mehmet get some breakfast on the go. The combination of gloomy weather and gloomy prospects dampened their spirits considerably. Aysha emerged and turned on the television in the corner for the news. She listened as the newsreader described the worsening diplomatic situation. Suddenly, she called out to the drivers. 'They are going to close all the Syrian borders,' she said. 'It's on the news. The government is preparing for one of America's "shock and awe" strikes.'

'We'll have to go, then,' Bingo said. 'We'd better get the show on the road straight after breakfast.'

'What are you going to do, Titania?' Eric asked.

'I don't know. I'll have to go back with you, I suppose. It'd be stupid to get trapped here, wouldn't it.'

'It would,' Bingo agreed. 'What about you, Ro?'

Fish, Fog, Fire and Fear

'I'm staying,' Ro said, flatly.

'You could come with us and return when it's all blown over,' said Bingo.

'No. Nuri will return here and expect to find me here, so I'm staying,' Ro said.

'They'll close the airport and Nuri won't be able to get into Syria anyway,' Eric said. 'Then you'll be in danger while he's safe in Saudi.'

'Or the reverse might happen; so I'm definitely staying here,' Ro insisted.

'At least this place seems to be out of their sights now that the military has gone,' Jumbo said, encouragingly. 'They'll attack military installations and perhaps parts of Damascus and the ports instead.'

'Let's hope Jumbo's right,' Bingo said doubtfully.

Farewells were finally said in the freezing fog that overlaid the compound. Each of them hugged Ro before climbing into a warm cab. Ro felt very small, withdrawing his head into his camel-hair wrap, as the three lorries began to make their way to the gate. It seemed to Ro that his life was fragmenting before his very eyes.

When they were gone, Ro walked slowly back to the domain feeling very flat. He could hear the muffled sound of the cock crowing. Still coughing from the diesel smoke, he busied himself around the place, stoking the kitchen stove and breaking the ice in the outside water dispensers. He heard the gate swing and he turned round. Kamal appeared out of the mist.

'Come on, Ro,' he said. 'Let's go and help at the factory. Some of it can be rescued.' The pair set off across the compound.

Exit Strategies

The three British lorries crawled out of the access road onto the old, Homs–Damascus highway and climbed the bleak-looking mountain through the fog. Bingo was at the front staring past the windscreen wipers, which had been turned to 'intermittent'.

'It's a bit snowier higher up, by the look of it,' Jumbo's voice said on the CB.

'It's bloody quiet,' Eric said. 'This road's usually busy night and day.' They climbed higher without seeing more than a trickle of cars going in the other direction.

'I hope they let us out through the border,' Bingo said into his microphone.

'They will,' Jumbo answered. 'At times like this, they usually want the foreigners out as quickly as possible. When Romania revolted, they couldn't get us out quick enough!' An escorted convoy of containers drove by in the opposite direction.

Eventually, they joined the newer motorway, which was just as quiet as the old road. 'Watch out up here, lads,' Bingo said, as they rounded a bend, 'there's a big snowdrift blocking the inside lane. We'll have to go round it.'

'Hang on, I've got a fuel problem!' Eric shouted. Bingo had already committed himself to the outside lane. He slowed down and looked in his mirrors. Eric's truck was slowing to a stop at the beginning of the drift. Jumbo pulled up behind him. 'We can't stop here!' Jumbo said.

'I can't go at all,' Eric shouted. 'If you drop back a bit I'll try and reverse back down into the nearside lane where the snow starts.' Three sets of hazard lights flashed on and off as they snaked back down the hill in reverse. 'I hope nobody comes up behind us, they'll never see us round the bend if they're going fast,' Eric said. 'Shit, the engine's cut out altogether! Now I've got no power steering. And there's a hell of a smell of diesel in here.'

They came to rest at the start of the snowdrift on the apex of the bend. Eric began to tilt the cab. Three cars came by at high speed, covering them with spray and narrowly missing them. 'I'll go back a bit and flag them, to slow them down,' Bingo said. 'They'll never see a warning triangle in this light.'

'There's an old lorry tyre down the hill a bit. Take some matches and a bag of rubbish and see if you can make a fire,' said Jumbo. 'You don't want to be flagging cars down in this light.'

'Empty those vegetables out of the wooden crate in my locker. That'll provide some firewood,' Eric said from where he crouched over the engine.

'How are you getting on, Eric?' Jumbo said when Bingo had gone.

'It's the feed pipe. It's chafing against the return pipe. They've both worn through. Have you got a length of hose, Jumbo?'

'That'll be that twat in the workshop,' Jumbo said. 'I should have done it myself.'

Bingo walked down the cold wet road and dragged the lorry tyre onto the carriageway. He managed to get a fire going but couldn't persuade the tyre to catch. A lorry passed. Then he saw flashing lights, and an army convoy rounded the bend. It came to a halt by Bingo, who pointed up the hill to Eric's tilted cab. The convoy proceeded slowly, then stopped again. By the time Bingo had walked back to the lorries, a group of mechanics had sized up Eric's problem and were scrambling about in the engine compartment with their sleeves rolled up. An hour later, the three English wagons were on their way again.

After about half an hour's driving, Bingo's CB crackled. 'I reckon the transit convoys must already have escorted the last foreigners out,' Jumbo said. 'There's not a Turk in sight.'

Towards Homs, the road became very wet with slush, but the fog lifted. When they got to the border at Bab al Hawa late that night, they found a long queue of lorries stretching right back into the countryside. They slept where they were.

Kamyonistan remained wrapped in fog. During the day, two convoys of containers arrived from Latakia. Ro was given a long list of trailers to move onto the TIR parking. The list included the

Iranian tilts and a dozen or so containers. 'Park them in a fairly haphazard fashion, Ro. Make them look as if they're ordinary trailers.'

'Aren't they ordinary trailers?' Ro asked.

'Of course, of course!' Fahmy replied. 'When they're all moved, perhaps you would pull that fridge off bay six and drop it in the service road just past the wall of the truck stop, will you?' Fahmy turned to a couple of other shunter drivers and gave them similar instructions.

Ro was suspicious. After moving the first five Iranian tilts, he went for a quick *shay* in the shunters' rest room. On the way out again, he noticed that the crates being loaded from one of the containers into the warehouse bore the international dangerous goods symbol for nuclear cargo.

He continued to move trailers until the light failed at the end of the afternoon. Then he dug another bit of garden before feeding the chickens and the camels. He visited the drivers' suq to buy food and supplies. Stocks were running low. Feeling anger mounting inside him, he walked to the restaurant. 'Don't look so dejected, Ro,' Mehmet said. 'Nuri will soon be home.'

'It's not that,' Ro said, sullenly. 'It's these bloody trailers!'

'What about them?'

'The compound looks as if it's a busy truck stop as usual,' Ro said.

'So?'

'There isn't a tractor unit in sight. No one who studies satellite pictures of Kamyonistan is going to be fooled by me parking trailers as if it's a normal Tuesday evening. They are obviously full of dangerous weapons,' Ro said, heatedly.

'Shush! Keep your voice down, Ro! You never know who might be listening.'

'I stayed because I thought this place was comparatively safe,' Ro protested.

'No you didn't, you stayed because of Nuri,' Mehmet retorted.

'Well, Kamyonistan is becoming as dangerous as it was before the rocket attack,' Ro said. 'We're sitting ducks! I only wish Nuri would come back soon so that we can get out of here.'

'Where would you go?' Mehmet said. 'You'd die on the mountain, and Damascus is not going to be a clever place to be when the shit hits the fan.'

Mehmet turned the television on. There were pictures of people panic-buying food. Then pictures of men fighting over tins in front of empty shelves were shown. Footage of military movements followed empty street scenes. Finally, real-time views of the blacked-out capital were shown. Ro watched shots of an airliner landing before the runway lights were killed. There followed a short address given by the President. Ro's mind raced. Nuri had almost certainly seen common sense and remained in Saudi Arabia. Perhaps he should have listened to Bingo after all. Suddenly, he felt really scared.

Restless, he returned home and made a light meal. He went into the garden. The fog was lifting and there was a veiled moon. From over the wall, he heard the sound of a trailer being unfastened. Ro froze. He realised that someone must be opening up the fridge that he had dropped there earlier. Scaling the Russian tilt, he climbed onto its roof and worked his way onto the wall. Crouching, he waddled as far as the roof of the camel shelter and peeped down. Astonishingly, a group of pack mules stood in the dull moonlight, their breath white upon the chilly air. A group of young men dressed in paramilitary clothes were unloading rifles and grenades from the trailer. At first, he thought the smugglers were pilfering, and it occurred to him to raise the alarm. Then he remembered that he had been instructed to park that trailer at exactly this vulnerable point. Fahmy must be in on this, Ro thought. He recognised a voice, then another. It dawned on him that these were the same young soldiers he had encountered earlier. Perhaps gunrunning was their real job and soldiering was just their day job, he thought.

A car swung into the road at the other end. The youths dived for cover as the headlights swept the road before the car turned into the truck stop. His foot tapped the roof of the shelter and the she-camel beneath, gave a loud hoot of protest. The smugglers looked up and one raised his rifle. 'Don't shoot, it's me!' Ro called.

The youths clustered below him. He sat on the wall, dangling his legs over the edge. 'You haven't seen us!' one of them said. Ro recognised him as the tall soldier, Karim.

'Are you going to Lebanon?' Ro asked.

'Come down!' the youth said. Ro began to scramble down the high wall and they all reached up to help him.

'What if we are going to Lebanon?'

'Won't it be dangerous?'

'It's always dangerous, but at the moment the army's too occupied getting ready for the invasion. The border area will be quiet in parts,' said Karim. Ro wondered if this was the soldier Mahmout had referred to.

'Take me with you,' Ro said, suddenly. 'I'll be careful.'

'We could do with your camel,' Karim said. 'It can carry a bit more than these mules.' He turned to the others. They looked doubtful, then scared. An argument broke out. Voices were raised and quickly quietened.

'They just want to take the camel, Ro,' Karim said, 'but I've reminded them that no one else here knows what to do with a camel. Bring as much food and water as you can. Wear warm clothes and a blanket. Meet us behind the south wall by the new access road in two hours. Then we'll move to a sheltered spot in the hills and leave at dawn. Pray for fog.'

Ro walked back and entered by the gate. He wondered what he would say to the gate man. Would he believe that Ro fancied a spin on the camel in the fog at this time of night? The gate man was not there, and neither was the policeman. A loose chain had been placed across the entrance. Ro supposed that, with no traffic, there was no call for a gate man. The car that had entered earlier approached from within the compound. It was a taxi. Ro obligingly raised the chain for it to pass underneath.

While he was packing and organising clothes, he remembered the baby camel. Angry with himself for overlooking this important element, he decided that it would just have to go with them. Ro thought of what he would write for Nuri in case he arrived at a later date. He wrote a note for Mehmet so that he would not think that Ro had been murdered or something. Then he opened the doors of the chicken coops so that the birds could get out and forage in the morning.

Upstairs, he placed the camel-hair wrap next to a woollen jumper on the bed and found some thick socks. Then he looked for a sharp knife and found a good pair of trousers with deep pockets. Next, he placed the soft saddlebags over the kitchen table and filled both sides with food and bottles of water. The door opened behind him and in walked Nuri. They embraced.

'Sirens!' Nuri said. 'I've just seen the television in the Janna. Damascus is blacked out, and the sirens are wailing.'

Border Crossing

Ro opened his eyes. He was stiff with cold. In the night he had slept fitfully under his blanket. Distant Kamyonistan remained intact. He was certain of this, for there had been no sound of an attack. Through the mist he could make out the dull brown of the rocks. Nuri was crouching over a small fire in which a kettle was already steaming. He arose with his blanket still round his shoulders and joined Nuri. Karim stirred, then leapt into action, gathering mugs and handing them to Ro.

'How was Saudi?' Ro whispered.

'Brilliant. I'm really glad I went. They want me to go more often,' Nuri said. 'They said that if you go on a hajj with me, you could stay in Jeddah too.'

One by one the young gunrunners arose and squatted round the fire. They breakfasted on bread and tea before loading the beasts of burden. Nuri urged Ro to lead the big camel so that he could coax the infant over the difficult terrain ahead. The she-camel was loaded with rifles instead of food. When all was ready and traces of the fire had been obliterated, the little caravan set off into the mist.

At first it was hard going. They covered the ground that Ro had previously ridden over. Then the path became a little easier. At sunrise they paused briefly. The baby camel was much more robust than they had expected. He even showed signs of enjoying his adventure. Everything was new to him. Later in the morning, when they stopped to make *shay* and give the animals a rest, the sun broke through. This alarmed Karim, who was relying on the mist to give them cover for as long as possible.

They cooked a stew at midday, using fresh vegetables and tinned meat. Ro and Nuri took this task on as a sign of gratitude for being allowed to travel with the group. Then they pressed deeper into the mountains. The group's policy was not to talk as they walked but to listen for any unusual noises. To the sound of muffled footfalls, as they progressed along the track, a sense of peace began to take root in Ro.

That night, they camped in a hollow while the fog gathered thickly round them. 'What are we going to do in Lebanon?' Nuri whispered. 'They're sliding into another civil war there. It won't be safe to stay.'

'At least we won't get air-raided,' Ro said.

'I wouldn't count on it,' said Nuri. 'If we're caught with this lot by the wrong side, we've had it! We'll be back to square one with our visas too. We have Syrian visas and work permits, but nothing at all for Lebanon. We won't get a stamp where we're crossing!' In the blackness of the night, they huddled together for warmth.

After breakfast the following day, they began to climb high into the hills. The snow was deep in parts and Nuri began to fear for the little camel. By midday, it was showing signs of exhaustion. The group took a long lunch break, in spite of the cold. By teatime they were descending again and the temperature rose slightly. Ro asked Karim about the weapons and where they were bound, but Karim would answer no questions concerning their mission. Ro wasn't certain whether the guns were to supply Syrian fighters based in Lebanon or for Hezbollah. For all he knew, they may have been destined for a contingent he had never heard of. The thought worried him, because if they were caught he would have to justify his actions. Gunrunning had not sounded so dangerous in Kamyonistan. Now, as they approached the Lebanese border in a clandestine arms smuggling operation, it did not sound so cosy. He expressed his fears to Nuri, who simply shrugged. 'We should have thought of that before we left,' he said.

At midday the following day, they stopped at a crude stone shelter high in the hills. 'We're in Lebanon,' Karim announced. 'We'll have to wait here for instructions. Someone will meet us.'

Towards the end of the afternoon, a pair of middle-aged men, each with two mules, appeared at the bottom of the slope and made their way towards them. Introductions were made, *shay* was poured and Nuri recharged the pots. Some heated discussion ensued. Ro could sense that they were at the centre of the dispute.

After further debate, Karim turned to Ro and Nuri. 'They say it's too dangerous to take you any further,' Karim said. 'They feel that not only are both of you liabilities, because as foreigners you stand out too much, but also that your camels are too much of an oddity here.'

'What are we to do, then?' asked Ro.

'These men will take your load on their mules,' Karim said. 'We'll camp here tonight. Then tomorrow you must go back the way we came. Khemis here will go back with you as a guide. We can spare a mule now that these Lebanese contacts have brought spare ones.'

'But Karim,' Ro said, blowing on his *shay*, 'what about the invasion?'

'It's off,' Karim said casually. 'It was all bluff, apparently, to put the wind up the Syrian President.'

'What? Just like that?' Ro said, incredulously.

'Well, I'll be buggered!' Jumbo said into his microphone as the British lorries climbed the steep hill to the Belen Pass and the road to Iskenderun in Turkey.

'I don't suppose it'll make an ounce of difference,' Eric said. He was following Jumbo up the hill. 'Syria will deliberately misinterpret the gesture as a withdrawal and make much political capital out of it.'

'Well, maybe it really is a climb-down,' Jumbo said.

'Where are we stopping tonight, lads?' Bingo shouted. 'Aksaray? Or are we going to make up for lost time and keep going till our tacho time runs out?'

'Aksaray!' Eric replied. 'All that sitting around at borders has worn me out.'

'Lazy sod!' Jumbo laughed. 'If the snow is bad going up Tarsus, we may be lucky to get that far at all!'

'Never mind,' Bingo said, 'at least we know that Ro is probably safely ensconced in his cabin at Kamyonistan, and that Nuri is probably in Saudi. Titania's been trying to phone them all day but she can't get through. She's fed up because she could have stayed there after all.'

'She can always fly from Istanbul,' Eric suggested.

Mehmet shook his head in disbelief at the news of the aborted invasion. 'If politicians stopped toying with our lives, I'm sure the world would be a better place!' he said to Aysha. He turned the sound down on the television.

'What about Ro and Nuri?' Aysha said.

'Give them a couple of days, they'll be back; that's if they don't get caught by a mountain patrol. I've had a word with Fahmy, who seems to know a lot about these things. He reckons the lads are in good hands.'

'I'll go and light their stove, then,' Aysha said. 'They'll want to come home to a warm house. I'll get Amoun to feed the chickens too. He shut them all up again yesterday after he found them wandering all over the compound.' She left, humming to herself.

The night before they reached Kamyonistan, Ro, Nuri and Khemis camped in a sheltered place. It had been necessary to stop early so as not to exhaust the little camel. Khemis announced that he would take his leave of them before dawn, as they were so close to their destination. He insisted that Ro and Nuri could easily manage the last hour without him.

They chatted until late, huddled under a pile of blankets. Khemis hinted that he was well connected in the transport zone and that Ro and Nuri would always be well protected there. Nuri perceived more than a passing likeness of Fahmy in his face and wondered if Khemis was his son. They talked about Ro's plans to keep goats. Ro gave a detailed account of the day the chickens were transferred to their domain. Nuri was keen to hear about the plot of land that Ro had dug over for vegetables. They began to form plans for an enclosed sanctuary like the mosque garden: a garden within a garden that the goats and chickens would not reach. Nuri suggested taking bougainvillea cuttings from the mosque and growing hibiscus flowers for the delicious drink, *kerkade*. When Ro and Nuri had looked up the word 'paradise' on the office computer they had discovered that it originated as *pairidaeza*, an old Persian word meaning 'walled enclosure', and that the word was associated with the Sanskrit word *paradesha*, meaning foreign country. One by one they fell asleep.

Enchanted Place

At dawn, Ro and Nuri arose and made *shay*. They smelt of woodsmoke, camels and sweat, but they knew that civilisation lay less than an hour away. As they set off, the fog began to lift. The camels lurched along the brown track and Nuri sang softly. When finally, they crested the last summit on the approach to the transport zone, the sun appeared brightly in the east, and there before them lay the most glorious sight. The creamy walls and minarets of Kamyonistan rose gloriously out of the mist, which boiled gently around it and rolled away into the mountains. They heard a distant cockcrow from their little domain. Ro fancied he could see a spiral of smoke rising from the cabin. While their camels stood placidly in the warming rays, the two boys surveyed the vision with wonder in their eyes and their hands met. Here was the location of their hopes and dreams; here was that enchanted place where the optimism of youth was strong. Here was Kamyonistan revealed in all its glory. They were home.

Printed in the United Kingdom
by Lightning Source UK Ltd.
135094UK00002B/1-18/P